VERTICAL LINE

By

Peter Preston

'Vertical Line' is dedicated to the memory of my mother.

Vertical Line

ISBN: 978-1-291-89684-8

Bloomsbury-Alpha Press
London, 2016
verticaline@hotmail.com

CHAPTER ONE

Sassafras stayed in the tower, burnt and broken; subject to pity, to strange omens. Defeated - the burden of the tower itself upon tormented shoulders - and the whisperings, sighings, the terrible cries of ordinary men.

Outside, the wooden slopes festered - grey, crumbling. The hasty edifice cast a long shadow, it touched dry earth but the tower itself glistened. The sun rose.

Sassafras, victim of misgivings, lord of little, begetter of nightmare, self-cursed; he whose story is not told, Sassafras the lost. Sassafras, without hope, gift of a starless night and vain seat of aspiration. Sassafras the teacher.

Sassafras, save us!

We have come from beyond rivers with our need and our hopelessness. We have crossed water, this nearest sea and the lakes in between. Nights without light, days in shadows, days under broad leaves, days in the damp, swamp days, vapour days, days with winds rising and some without accustomed repose. We have eaten from burrows.

Sassafras, teach us!

Our company has grown. Misshapen, erect, we take on the

forms of our dearest wishes. We catch at the light.

Sassafras' wishes were visible in this dawn's rays. Partial forms. But for the glimpse that we sought there was need for close attendance, the acceptance of one other's dominion.

Sassafras! Look down on travellers, on halting attempts, on our struggles.

The sun lit the valley. Across the widest gulf red rays stretched - mist-etched, bright, they caught at dust motes and on the banks at brilliants; and at the sparkle of dew. The leaves rustled. Few noises could be heard. Across the gulf some tinkling - an early worker, the working of metal, the movement of animals. We caught sight of the water tumbling, trickling, falling the hundreds of paces. We looked to where it dipped to the abyss - to the dark that lay below the unaccustomed regions where the sun never shone. It shone on Sassafras' tower.

Sassafras' work had filled a number of years. Hampered by scarcities, unaccountable losses, natural disadvantages which attend disfigurement, a certain distance, disdain, the lack of interest of his companions; Sassafras worked alone. Sassafras' efforts were once caught between the needs of his helpers and his own rarest aspiration. Often he had faltered in his ambitions and in his work.

But some part of the edifice was completed. The tower reached a small way and falteringly he was raised just a little above the struggles and blindnesses of normal men.

Such was Sassafras' achievement.

Sassafras, teach us!

The wooden slopes of the building - moss-covered, mildewed, worn by the pressure of supplicants' hands, dried in the sun and twisted by frosts, rain, the butting of wild animals; forced by insect attack into a continued cycle: destruction, replacement, the eating and burrowing away. Replacement. Stolen from and subject to natural decay and that brought about maliciously, the slopes of the building had survived and held

Sassafras safe within. Safer by far than we could be, for our journey to this point had been through the perils of forests, vast distances, the sea and alien hordes. We had come to this point arduously.

Within the tower, Sassafras looked down. The teacher stepped forward and back, never ceasing to move agitatedly and forever changing, removing, increasing or displacing parts of his handiwork. He had worked so long and ceaselessly that rest was impossible. We were made aware that such achievement was the result of pleasure and of pain. Joy and sorrow were in its spire and castellations. There was anguish in its sloping wooden sides.

The face of the worker appeared above us. Behind a balustrade it disappeared once more and the noise of his working continued. Each blow, each sliding movement echoed, it filled the brightening valley.

The features of the teacher's suffering showed in the twisting of his architecture, the imbalance of his design. Each abandoned turret, each aborted pinnacle or fissure showed moments or years when pain had caused Sassafras to cease to care.

Many stories were told - in the regions through which we had passed - of the pattern underlying this building, the tower: that its design could be uncovered if one's approach and one's feelings corresponded to some part of its builder's. For the most part and to most of our number the tower was a thing of mystery - shrouded in mists, rising, faltering, branched and perplexing. Moistened and eroded at the same time; heaped about with the remains of former essays: with doors, lintels - whole rooms worked in oak or some other durable material - trials and models for the perplexing inner structure. There were clues all around, they were everywhere to be seen.

Sassafras looked down.

Sassafras looked down, caught amid the trappings of his own

desires. He looked from inside some study - perhaps gilded with curlicues representing each of the fates yet to befall its creator; perhaps from inside some observatory - a bronze and iron room filled with instruments and lens systems, with heavy volumes of tables and with charts covering every wall. This room would be crowded with the remains of those devices near completion and of the observing mirrors, recorders and artefacts designed to penetrate perhaps the mist in the valley below, or perhaps to give warning of the hundred dangers which beset the tower and the builder of the tower. By his efforts alone could Sassafras be safe.

And this was to be the first of all such lessons: for when expressed so physically, the spirit - soaring - must be protected. This fine expression is vulnerable. To rise higher it must be cosseted, consolidated, it must be held from special attack and the rooms, walls, buttresses, the stairwells and heavy oak furniture - Sassafras' expression, the working of years - held dreams and could lead elsewhere.

The teacher looked down. Tremors ran to and fro. We caught at our breath.

"Sassafras! Teach us!"

He drew himself up. The clouds passing overhead, the small trees and rocky outcrops, the brightening horizon; Sassafras speaks:

"I have been able, on occasion, to see events in the far region."

"Yes."

"I have seen those lights and bright towers which are partly hidden . . ."

"Tell us. Tell us!"

"And the light thoroughfares, some glimpse of the life in them: the people move in sympathy, I have caught sight of them when rare communication passes between them. I have seen them during their contemplation, when gesture, feeling, movement become one and pride, joy, delicacy and the awareness of whispers pass among them.

"Their world is beautiful with the sun, with other light, the brightness of aspiration. For these, the uncountable faults and obstacles are passed swiftly so that the imagination grasps only some small part, some lower vibration of what upper tones must actually be theirs."

Just then thunder sounded. The light marking this dawn became suddenly grey. The raindrops splashed between leaves, making small sounds on grass and shrubs where they fell. At the sound, a shiver passed through our number. It vibrated between the figures, it ran forward and back catching at the worn and misshapen faces of travellers and sufferers: the Victor Over Every Misfortune, the Beautiful Seeker, the Family and the others.

This terror was able to grow. It leapt huge gaps, eventually making for the open space and it rushed towards the tower - over short grass and small shrubs, by ditches and over small humps and little depressions. It sped faster and faster, and made straight for the tower. It broke there shaking the wooden walls and bringing forth showers of light, it collided with the tower's light that descended from the bright face of the teacher, it fractured the moment in white, in purple; in vermilion. This instant shifted, from the base of the tower both black and white radiated - white fringes processed. The fingers shot out aiming for low projections. Crossing ridges and island shrubs - scarring and wounding - flying outward from the tower, flying outward from wooden walls and carrying with them dark fragments.

They shot outwards. The fragments leapt in arcs into the air, they cut through treetops and brought down leaves and small branches.

The white fingers knuckled, they broke to form brilliant spheres and these spun outward instead. They ran scorching through the shrubs and short grass. They collided in showers of light with tree roots and stumps. Extinguished, they set red flames to blackened wounds. As fires sprang up the last shimmering orb ran between us. It burned, it maimed; this lightning stopped, turned, twisted, caught first at this leg and then blinded that traveller. For the moment of its life it was terror - a last avenger, reaper, the burning sword.

Finally stilled, it floated poised beneath undergrowth and a group of small shrubs. Here it span slowly, caused the branches to ignite, and, becoming totally translucent, vanished altogether. The eyes of all who saw it remained dazzled by its light.

Our group stared. Fair Union lay still on the ground, Perception and Hope reached across to each other blackened and burned. The eyes of Final Journey were fixed on the sky. He lay transfixed by the shard that had ended his life.

The terror cries began. All around the fires raged. Beautiful Seeker smothered flames with garments and beat at springs of flames with branches. The Victor pulled at his companions and dragged them carefully to safety.

As the fires raged higher we huddled in a knot. The smoke from all around filled most of the sky and certainly covered the tower. We turned to our dead and wounded.

Fair Union, she who cared for us when wounded by forest creatures and sickened by the plague swamps, she who carried all on her shoulders and loved but was not loved - loved emptily - is dying. Her eyes flicker and the breath stops, starts again, falters. She breathes out the names of her loved ones now gone, and she is gone. She is still and blood trickles slowly staining the ground.

And Final Journey, decked out in amulets and souvenirs – mementoes of his solitary passage through mountains and of his journey before he joined our number (he would sing us to sleep on many nights with songs of earlier ventures) - Final

Journey was dead.

But Perception and Hope lived and they fought for the others and for themselves. While gathered round these forms and sheltering from the flames we wished and we hoped, we cursed the heavens for their strange attack. The sky itself moved liquidly and black shapes recoiled overhead. Our cries reached the dark branches above and, attaining these, floated beyond through drifts of smoke, through ashes and sparks; the flowing, twisting leaves that hung in the air. They drifted above these trees and over the valley, they reached to the tower where Sassafras stood and where, if wishing, he could look down at the scene of scorched and terrified travellers; at scorched and burned grass, trees; the smoking small crater at the foot of the tower, the paths that the fiery spheres took in their sudden wanderings; and the single fiery track scarred on the tower - scarred from the very topmost reach of the tower down by castellations, wall and buttress to the ground. From where he now stood to the battered cavity at the foot of the edifice - the crater and the wooden fragments - Sassafras' tower was now partly broken. The stairways were exposed and impassable in places.

This was clearly only the latest such destruction, for it obscured the damage caused by a host of other misfortunes. It cried out to the tumbling skies as the green fragments of mosses and mildewed wood fell from charred beams; it was one further attack on the aspiration of the creator.

The lord of this misfortune stood at the top of his tower, stood where both achievement and destruction would be visible at any glance, stood at the pinnacle of both and gestured to speak.

Sassafras' voice was hardly audible: the teacher's words continued but like the tearing at the tower, the shuddering of thunder broke his speech. While his voice continued and his eyes never flickered, the thunder reverberated so that words were fragmented and were now made meaningless. Nothing of what he said could be heard.

But Sassafras continued. Neither looking down on the destruction nor faltering in his exposition, he continued, and as we shivered below at the frightful thing that had befallen us, as we held our dead and wounded fellows close and sheltered ourselves fearfully, it was Sassafras, lord of broken aspiration, Sassafras the teacher whom we attended.

Sassafras' brilliant eyes looked straight ahead, the sound of metalwork in the valley below broke out again, the wind rose and clouds shifted. Bright daylight fell on trees, on the slopes and in light patches which moved rapidly over them.

The morning sun rose higher still. It lifted over the trees and caught delicately at bright towers glistening in the far distance.

CHAPTER TWO

The Victor Over Every Misfortune gathered his nearest friend to him and lifted Hope and Perception too. Sadly we lifted up Fair Union and Final Journey. We moved to the lower slopes where the soil was lighter, where there was shade for their graves and where the burning air had not yet reached so that they could lie removed from the stench of their destruction. The teacher behind us was silhouetted against the sky.

The grass was soft, the slope became steeper. Green saplings caught at the clothes, the hair and at the burdens we were carrying. Cries of the wounded rang out as each branch and each sapling tore at burnt and bleeding wounds.

At the graveside our cries drifted to the valley.

"We have come a long way," Wisdom said. He threw earth onto Final Journey's form.

"And these friends have undertaken so very much," the Victor whispered. The mound grew higher.

"From their homes by the ocean and several in the mouths of rivers the companions of these friends gathered. For myself, when I lived in the swamp lands I knew there would be a fine and shining point somewhere. And when we met - Fair Union and I - our efforts produced some sweeter balance, though for Final Journey I knew I could understand just a small part of his actual goal."

Wisdom drew away.

Perception, fighting pain and the weakness of loss, raised herself on one arm. She knew, she felt, something of Final Journey's aim.

"He was given," she said, "to the strangest of ideas. Once he had described the fall of rain and the inside of an oak tree. The tree, however, was so large he could move freely within.

"Water fell on the leaves and caused fine rivulets to coalesce where branches met or the trunk was encountered. In the tree, however, he remained dry. The light from the opening struck across the cavity and caught at speckles of rain, dried leaves, the wood's smoothed inner texture. It warmed where it touched.

"And wood thrives on such care. He was able to see the way in which it grew so that, in the smallest of stages, the tree increased from within. And the smoothness of the wood surrounded him, new wood caressing him, so that each finger became held gently and water-fed growth surrounded all his limbs.

"In this way he was part of the tree growth and part of the work of falling rain. He felt great joy and wholeness when the light from above was finally broken off and rich sturdy wood penetrated his body completely. This tree was thus able to prosper."

Fair Union evinced an equal sympathy. Her raised grave was alongside its fellow but had not yet reached as high. For travellers like us her encounter held very rare memories.

The wind rustled the leaves above our heads. It gusted admonishingly. Fair Union had contributed her love this way, unexpectedly. On that occasion, not alone as she imagined, she had run among the trees. Small animals and the tall stranger were joyfully disturbed.

First Leader has told us how her strange fears began. Eyes stared at leaves dislodged, at the drifting, wind-blown folds in clothes. He told of her gestures - enquiry, entreaty, and the different hope that grows on unexpected meeting.

Fair Union spoke of her burdens. The words shimmered. She was able to reach out too, not knowing any name, silenced in fact in her enquiry, and by gesture show her welcome and her happiness.

First Leader spoke brightly of other reaches of the forest, took her arm, pointed, led off and they moved silently through small avenues and into clearings and under high trees with giant trunks.

And the moving canopy and the lower branches which reached down from great heights came close to the ground. They made their passage difficult, perhaps brushing their faces as they walked.

The Leader took Fair Union's hand, spoke gently and at once she was dazzled by the forest's beauty, the brightness of the sun's rays, the fine dance of the motes in light beams and the suddenly loud presence of insects and small animals.

And from this searching came some understanding so the strange fears shone in First Leader's eyes too. Thus approached, each of our number had swiftly moved. We advanced between rocks and the sea, along ridges of high mountains and from the depths of burrows. From the flight of insects we moved easily.

In this way the beginning of our association was greatly marked. Later, on walks through the forest, she whispered his name.

So, drawn on by strength, rare beauty, we had moved between fears. We had run from insect attack and cries of birds eating at night. A bright light had driven Fair Union in all her actions. From her forest love came the reason for our happy combination. Final Journey, his union with something living, and Fair Union's meeting with a helper were just such beautiful events.

Wisdom moved towards the centre. We gestured that the graves were complete and the funeral meditations too. The rain fell on stooped heads and wetted scorched clothing. We moved silently away.

The ring of metal sounded. A rainbow stretched a vapour path across the valley. The sun which now shone picked out the green of the valley floor and the higher swaying trees to each side. Low settlement roofs glistened. The river sparkled now and then in moments of bright sunshine and low mists filled the valley drifting, holding close, swirling - at places rushing fast and clear. We looked from Sassafras' tower into a green abyss warming in the sun and at times loud with circling winds.

In the valley was the low-walled settlement. The metal sounds came from below. The sun glinted from bright windows. Sparks of light caught in walls and masonry and played over smooth metal: parts of spades, the hinges of a gate, metal trowels. These sparkling lights radiated from an abandoned plough, the corners of buildings and water rivulets tumbling down the rocks and through the centre of the town. The river fell in giant leaps. It cascaded between rock outcrops covered in moss, by caves and hollows beyond remotest paths. In the great fall from the broken tower to the buildings below, the sparkling river moved left and right behind boulders, dividing, swallowed at times into rock channels - welling later into springs, rock pools and meanders. Swirling then unseen into underground ways with grass, twigs and small flowers that twisted - floating from higher reaches - this river then flowed between gravels.

The nearest bushes parted. Before us, with darkened faces, stood leather-clad figures. From their fellows behind came the scrape of metal on stone as they dragged steel chests towards the graves. Their faces were agitated. They mouthed unspoken words, they pointed work-worn hands and gestured fiercely. These first figures moved through us with burdens and less agitated movements which indicated the tower; that these newcomers wished to help in any distress and that they could aid our wounded. They invited the rest of us to help in scaling the height.

We recoiled immediately: the exposure of intimacy, the strangeness and the shock stilled us. We did not move. Instead, Wisdom took up our feeling: tremors ran through his frame and we, set in sympathetic motion, saw that another balance was established and that the company ought therefore to move on. Workers surrounded us on all sides.

"We must help at the tower!"

But the good souls had not seen Sassafras' face, they had not heard him speak gloriously. We indicated that we would not come. The rough, kind faces all around froze: fine chords snapped.

Wisdom spoke: "Friends, the tower struck by lightning has withstood other, terrible assaults.

"After the attack it was we, ignorant of this region, who were injured even killed - Sassafras, the teacher, considers none of these matters: he will arrange all things to preserve what is important. The present attack will have affected the teacher only to the degree he has shown - and we have seen him on the parapet of the tower, we have heard him speak (never pausing for anything: a bird in level flight, the rise of this sun). Nothing which was not equally ordered could disturb his excellent speech. We have learnt this much from him."

And the workers seemed this grateful too. They joined our celebration of the wisdom of our teacher, they told of other travellers and the joy that these came to know. They gestured lightly and talking rapidly of the other regions took us carefully to the village below.

CHAPTER THREE

We approached the smallest houses by dark. So rare were travellers here that every villager, approached unexpectedly, clawed at our hands and when strangely we were moved onward, broke down, clutched at garments and even struggled on the ground to come nearer.

Yet the metal workers were unmoved. So high was their standing among these others that none flinched or showed emotion. Throughout the afternoon they had described their work, the hopes that inspired their work and the glorious tasks that they performed amid the heat, the sound, and with the gentle assistance of the villagers.

Some of the metal workers were still at their tasks and from the centre of the village the sound of smelting, quenching and the pounding of hammers rang out. A small amount of smoke held to the centre of the town. We passed by low walls and through occasional arches. This early evening was alive and it was warm. Small moths flew at lights in open doorways, distant cries ran through passages and narrow streets. The streets themselves: mud brick, grey and brown with dust and broken pottery; the turnings of metal heaped in the corners and piled up to low windows; small lamps swinging from iron wall-baskets catching the moths - and the smell of animals and the sound of dogs barking - barking and picking at dry dust heaps and worrying each other and children in the street; and the children playing in the street, playing where light cuts outward from open doorways, children not yet awed by us but awed by the mothers, fathers; the crying and the joy in their faces; the rending of these people's clothes and the gentle, fervent cries. We passed through alleys with small houses, houses with doors and shutters wide open and families on the steps so that certain eyes followed us as we went onwards towards the metal foundry.

By the factory lay large boxes and chests of metal. They were bound in brass, they formed stacks and at places small, rust pools crept from their corners. The earth was stained with red and the walls of the long building, scratched, scarred, showed marks from other ironwork that lay there and had perhaps caught at the imagination with its fine curlicues, its delicate forms and elegant function.

Their work was surely excellent. In the fine turns and smaller features, in the closely honed jointings each metal piece showed all the skills and cares of hundreds of workers. Each reflected the greatest variety of needs. Indeed, only occasionally could some piece be understood to be a water-clock or the removable steps to a harrow or a plough. For the most part, the iron forms had about them some fine turning function or else the delicate motion of the writing hand. At times these forms were recognisable: parts from the familiar waterwheel, the loom, movable workings of clocks, so that engines as a whole grew in strangely mixed forms and their actual purpose remained shrouded, obscure. But when such functions did become clear, yet more aspects of the machines could then be discovered so that no more would the loom or the waterwheel be seen even as a part at all. Throughout, the metal workers would indicate by sign and gesture aspects meriting special attention. Some of what they said helped, certainly they were able to point to similarities and draw parallels between whole groups of devices. They spoke proudly, they gestured wildly and they pointed to the inside of the factory where pieces completed and some being worked on stretched into the distance, even disappearing in far reaches in haze or behind columns of massed ironwork.

We stood there amazed. Our guides, work-worn, tired, now in good spirits, had told us only a small part of the story of this towering work and now showed not a sign of that other strain which must come from the development of such ideas. As we walked towards the factory door the other villagers crowded round us, picked at our clothes and pulled us back. The Victor was held almost forcibly.

Without any other sign, the villagers began entreaties and a low moaning. As we walked into the darkness their voices were raised, only to die away when the last of us was lost to view. They then gathered round the long building, they beat at its walls and although any one of them could have walked in through the same entrance, crossing the courtyard, passing stables and the well used by the smelters, they did not and instead circled the building, made their protestations and did not cross the threshold or enter the darkness within. Their shadows formed a line by the great wooden doorway.

This last sight, gesturing villagers, despairing souls, fixed us as we all looked around peering into the dark, smoke-filled space, peering past the assembled work-pieces and on towards island lights: the bright sparkling, roaring fires that filled the factory, filled the space to the rafters with smoke and obscured our view of all but the nearest metalwork and the more obvious designs.

We walked further inside. By now we were out of the reach of the villagers and they, cowering, moved round the building for some time. Occasionally, they were to be seen at a window but generally they only caught the eye as they moved away. They were then seen leaving the fumes and the smoke of molten metal, returning to their homes disconsolately; and whispering briefly among themselves, the word *stranger* never being far from their lips and their backward glances betraying fear greater than anything else.

We wanted to know the reason for this fear, for the villagers' strange regard for the travellers in their midst, and we wanted to understand more of the great design of the metal workers.

We turned to their leader. This man, his face browned and with burnt and torn leather on his clothes, rushed forward and back. He held in one hand a projecting counterweight, turned it and made some point of explanation to the nearest traveller or metal worker; rushed across an aisle between large pieces and pointed to a divided rack - a recording device holding water in buckets and with iron rollers in balanced trays. Caught between the two, he glanced back at us all, ran instead to a smaller work-piece, made some further explanation and compared each artefact pointing to variations in function, to different methods of manufacture and to certain delicacies of design. One indeed, seeming more refined still, held our attention and the leader's too, for he grasped it in places, caressed traceries and curving blades and swept us into reveries about its strange function; the acclamation it would receive and the bright opportunities thus opened. The far regions would in one way be transformed by this handiwork - all of it too subtle for us at first to appreciate - and, should we stay in the territory, this device would of necessity touch even us.

We cast about ourselves to discover more. We ventured into deep recesses, we examined high archways, vaulted pillars and long passageways.

The pillars stretched into the darkness and each one housed a furnace. Along each aisle there moved a molten, gleaming stream. Metal workers grouped behind the furnaces forged, annealed, moulded. They gestured their directions, bound by a communion which owed nothing to their speech, for this was brief, brittle and held hardly anything of their more delicate meaning, their subtle, suggested variations; the gentle, finely perceived essence of their work. And yet with this pleasurable language delicate tasks were performed. The engines and machinery grew - without reference to plans, without a single worker pausing for advice or instructions; for the onset of doubts. Instead they moved smoothly, carrying pieces between furnaces, measuring and adjusting, fitting and testing until whole edifices were able to grow singly in front of us. They grew swiftly with other new processes of manufacture. While still hot in some places the work was tested and the driven force, the smiles and efforts of these workers never ceased, they performed their tasks with joy, joy centring on one or perhaps many bright ideas.

And we knew that outside mists might gather: that just one figure would look down. For some great part of these efforts had been started by a wonderful teacher. The first such worker had created plans and transformed this village. In the earliest days this foundry - which had rung with the sound of his raised hammer, his footsteps, the occasional drawing of water - had first been formed in one wonderful mind. And now this author was able to look down on our gentle meeting. With the last light fading, giving a final glimpse of the entrance, we were able to see the broken and deformed shape of the tower above. Where violet and deep dark-blue ranged above the shifting line of the swaying trees, the form of the tower stood clearly. It cut into the dark sky. It pointed upward to lights - sparkling in points - stars sparkling in points, glinting through these mists and poised above the trees; the swirling cold dark vapours from the trees; woods filled with small animals in their flight; dew-covered leaves, some needle-sharp and others weighed down;

dripping barks; the cries of the night birds.

The night vibrated. This chord now intoned from the tower at the head of the valley: charged night. And the mist which swirled from the height brought with it the teacher's differing sweet hopes. The mist drifted over burning air through the small ravines and the tumbling river, the river and smaller streams in hollowed rock paths, rock falls - where no steps are ever made and where only gentle wood sounds could be heard - and occasional distant hammering of metal.

These small concealed places had been in Sassafras' mind all of the time. When he fashioned the first of all metal structures he saw clearly these different dark images. Driven into the twisted delicate iron and in the turning cams and beautifully made shafts and cylinders are memories of dark cave mouths, these small ravines and the regions of the valley woods where the sun never shines and where strange forms are at times seen and where the sounds if they may be heard at all come distantly from the river.

And these distant images spurred the teacher all the time. The shapes which move in the trees resemble the trees. They have moved Sassafras in his search so that since such time he has begun rarer work still.

The town's air is burning. Above the small spires and low castellations, within this small reach, the air rises to the mist. With this burning ascent, the gaze of our sufferers will be cast upward. Beautiful Seeker's eyes now follow the turn of this heated air. He penetrates the cold of the abandoned, shrouded images, these mysteries of former journeys and of days in his trials in the warm fever swamps and the high winds of many mountains.

The warm air had drifted from around his heavy limbs, from beneath the plague mists; and thus he was able to stand erect, reach up and feel no fear that he would breathe in contagion and the fluid plague vapours that oppressed him for so many nights in the darker territories.

At that time, he could see the drifts which came no higher than he was, which reached upward but left the high ground free too - and the sparkling distant mountains, the light of the moon on their slopes and the shift of the mist layers; an airborne sea and a foetid cloud.

The aerial river flowed through the moonlit highland, it surrounded and covered trees, it tainted and disturbed those things living and it dipped here and there where water stood freely or rose from cracks in the ground.

Forking paths were obscured by this vapour layer, the light from the night sky was made dappled, it was made nauseous by the mist. And Beautiful Seeker, no longer constrained to dread and his fearful crawl, was able to see some way ahead of him; by bowing his head avoid his ceiling of vapours and edge a way forward out of the terrifying lower regions, so that when the moon rose fully above the twisted landscape he could look for his safe path, even rush for turbulent openings to the upper air and then in a sickly way make for smooth bluffs that might divide the valley's aerial flow.

On one such grassy spur he took breath at last.

Below him now vapours formed the stifling river. Alone and only able to guess at his companions' fates, he gloried in the free air that now surrounded him. At times, persisting slightly in garments, the smell of the sickness would taint the night. All the while, Beautiful Seeker's friends had not been as fortunate as he for, trapped, they still struggled to reach their high land too. Thus the night was rent with their despair - and Beautiful Seeker's desperate calls.

They died that night. The Seeker, succeeding to their aims and pacing his refuge, waited in the high night air, in the moon's chill - pacing the rocks above the white sea, and through the night.

When morning came the Seeker was standing looking toward

the sun. For hours looking to the spot where the red rays would begin, he trembled with the cold, with anticipated fears and with revulsion at the poisonous sea reaching upwards, curling about the lower rocks and engulfing, colouring and obscuring everything beneath. It obscured dear forms: the bodies of friends and companions and it held him captive on this island of the night sky.

The red rays touched his refuge. The morning moved clouds from beneath him, showed him at last the swamps through which he had stumbled and brought back the images of the terrible pursuer and the sight - now and then - of the remains of his friends.

He began judging the moments when gaps parted in the breeze. Soon, between wraiths of this poison, over humped rocks and finally on the stones of the paths forking and crossing over the swamp lands he picked a delicate way from the sounds of his pursuer, and the sight of discarded human bones. He moved toward flatter lands.

The swamps and other obstacles beset each of our number. The forests and rivers of far territories were often unknown; their traps, elaborately set, held so many back that only fortunate ones could come this far and among those only some felt as we did, joining - with a little joy - our adventure.

Beautiful Seeker looked out of the high arched window at this night's mist. The metal workers - now carrying some large work-piece, now quenching it in tubs to the sound of issuing steam, and then perhaps turning some small part on a lathe until finally examining the burnish on delicate moving parts - these workers at times indicated to Beautiful Seeker's enquiring gaze the mountain tops and the tower, the rising mist and the forests which covered these mountains as if Sassafras, his vision, the work now being executed and the far regions were only parts of something more; were perhaps spreading further still.

But only some could see. In this way, those wanderers that

we had each passed before the first encounter, each of these souls had seen just one part of what might lie before our eyes. These friends had found that other lights shone out brightly. They had found that the gift of mists and of stars in the day was bright where they were then able to see, that our crystal light fell short in some detail and that our gentle messengers produced a less happy reaction.

For each of us, a first encounter was to be desired. And when this at last occurred, stars and the moment shimmered before us. We moved through each separated hardship. Later we were to meet under the whispering shade of a welcoming tree.

And we each spoke:

Friend loved bright grasslands. She had scattered small-life before her. This vision persisted. It filled the sun, it moved winds between the grasses and sent insects scuttling. Friend walked through flat and wide grasslands by day. She strode out; never beyond the company of the bright grass maidens - those bearing fruit of the grasslands - she progressed and these helpers ran by her side, caught at her clothing and gathered about her hopefully. The maidens brought forth gentle rain, sun and the cover of the clouds.

These helpers had known Final Journey, could relate events of his union, felt such kinship with this figure of the tallest trees and longed for discourse with one - such as he - a traveller.

Garlanded, slight, the maidens danced as Friend walked (also beautiful: her hair was caught up with blooms and medallions of other travellers, several lovers; of the lords of the high rocks above them - and the people of the far regions). They kept her spirits high for through this territory had occurred terrible pursuits and the swathes of grass were crossed by paths made by men and animals hunted and desperately running. They ran to reach the rocks of the mountains above.

This land was green and sun-warmed. Thought of such

fearful events came only slowly to their minds. They slept with the dreams of torment; of faces caught fleetingly by reflections from a fire; of forest faces and the images in stone at the bottom of the stream - cold water faces, threats and visions from the silences beneath the water, from high on the rocky prominences and from the depths of caves.

Sassafras! From the purple depths of these mountain caves deliver us! From the open black mouths beneath your tower guard and save us. We have come hopefully, from distant terrors and through dangers not yet dreamed of. Show us the way in which to hope.

The disturbing sounds of water in cave depths, dripping, had caught us as we moved downward from the tower (carrying burdens with the metal workers, carrying their chests as we moved from the heights) - at that time not really aware of the beautiful plans and fighting back terrible fears. In these caves, near the tumbling river, were hints of our past trials and in the water which flowed from the largest cave (the still pool and the largest tributaries) were visions of the fine human tree, Fair Union's forest love and our teeming dream - torment, other men's lives.

This prospect became confused, breaking and forming at the pebbles and rocks in the cave's mouth. The images wove and coalesced before the water and its fragments curled on their way - slight moments and small visions that fall and glint in the evening air – that reflect the warm evening sky, the purple of night and the sparkling brilliants; their stars and the vapour rising from the warmed trees, the gentle night sounds and the tumble of this water over pebbles, these broken visions, gentle hopes, the distant reflections of our kind.

The grass maidens kept distant dark images; they raised hope above the fear of desperate chases, above the cold water faces and the broken cave forms which howl into the night and cry out to the dark life surrounding us.

25

The invention of Sassafras, this work in the village and his later tower, the aims of metal workers and the fine efforts of the travellers all suggest regions far away and, indicate too, the forest, swamplands and strong union with trees. As sparks rise from the foundry (a torrent, a rising luminous cloud) we all of us straight away thought brightly of the future greatest task of all.

CHAPTER FOUR

Above the valley mists circled. Over the small buildings and mingling with the heated air, the clouded air obscured small shrub-trees and the ruined pathways. The trees rustled.

Large shapes arose, they twisted. Above in the night air they cut off the moon.

The wind moved in the trees, rounded and turned inward. The shapes swirled: first one cloud and then the stars were obscured. The forms were bright, translucent, and their colours tinged the stars seen through them. Red, purple, the light from the stars struck outward. It moved, stabbed downward. Finger-rays circled in the night with these shapes.

Whipped by the wind, they turned and the eye became dazzled by striking rays. Sparkling light progressed along columns. They turned and scintillated. The sparks within columns streaked outward, changed in hue.

The turning vision delicately raised hope. The dream flashed light outward and illuminated in this way the banks of the valley, shrub pathways, small caves, the torrent and rivulets.

In the night sounds reverberated, they echoed into open mouths and such visions caught in the caves, becoming held there, twisted in the rocks and so spun underneath us all.

In the earth lay the remains of lower animals.

Sassafras heard the gentlest cries. The vision flitted through sandy streets to the walls of the foundry, onto the path of the river, over boulders, gravel, grass, and the earth between small outcrops. It twisted the air above; below the earth voices could be heard. These cries from hopeful ones rang from the village. The hopes of each villager were able to cause fractures in the earth. Descending then, they sprung open cave roofs and the passages of water that moved underground.

New water surfaces seen through cracks in the ground glistened. Our vision rippled in darkened water and the arcs, rays and moving brilliants - the circling form - became reflected in the new cavern walls. It shimmered there.

We were distracted by the admirable light. The broken voices underground cried out for us to beware, that the slight and moving shadows were not what they seemed and that dazzling rays reached fissures in the skin, the blemishes and the cankers within.

"The rays will disturb, they will deform areas unseen."

But still, what were these broken cries when the blessing of the wheeling, opalescent vision fell upon us, when we were carried up in the transport of its desire? And the earth shifted all the while.

The wind rose. Sassafras' vision was delicately threatened. We saw in the distance the spare figure as it climbed down the ruined side of the tower. Flashes passed from one part of the horizon to the broken building, the whole world was thus periodically made white and the progress of the dreamer down the tower's outer wall was seen as jerky, for he would leap down from the remains of one floor level to another, yet wander for quite long periods at each before the way to descend further became visible. With the flickering horizon behind him, his progress seemed assured.

He reached the ground at last. It seemed important, at the end of his climb, to know of the teacher's direction but he disappeared and we were left with feelings of being alternately trapped and then abandoned.

There was anger about. The very light which had merely illuminated now sent sharp rays and tremors outwards and we felt the waves flowing down to the village, to the tower and the hillsides and depths below the slopes. This shape now vibrated horribly. Least of all could we travellers withstand the vibrant rays now turned deeply hostile and the violet of this illumination sent us seeking shelter wherever the shadows were deepest, from which hiding places we looked out to see next where it might penetrate and wither.

We huddled together. Travellers and some of the villagers - though almost all of these working people were presently at tasks as near to the foundry as possible - these people cried out. The houses, vibrating to the harsh rhythms, shuddered and large pieces became detached. The shaking of the earth now opened underground streams and they flowed out where roads and the foundations of buildings were. Screams could be heard from stairwells and the cellars of the town and from the foundry, amid the crash of machinery and the scorching fires. We grappled with broken branches and a flood.

What great mystery was this that laid waste the schemes of Sassafras and the love of these people?

We ran from the flames and flood, from the whirling image that hung overhead, from the last hope and the threat to this distant dreamer and we ran into the night where these shapeless forms could be familiar, where caves opened wide and the fractures opened, too: to engulf and to absorb our living friends.

We ran on. Trees fell in our path. Crashing before us they would move just as other red cracks might open in the earth. We ran fearfully and leaped over fissures forming and rushed between broken limbs of trees. Many times Sassafras' tower had been similarly attacked. We crossed the river. As the earth shifted we made for the largest rock standing above the town: a solid mass which by day cast shadows into the streets, by night blocked out the stars. We ran up the broken side. Through wet grass and above fractured rocks we dragged ourselves up - cut and bleeding - into its lee and into shelter from the burning light above. The darkest mouth beckoned us inward.

Our skin became seared. The violet rays that dazzled the eyes covered delicate skin with night burns and sent heat shimmering all over the body. Under the clothes the skin scintillated and the air close to it became charged. Small irritations shimmered to and fro.

With the eyes now burning and heat pricking at the air we ran blindly to the only certain shade from the fierce night rays. While we could yet see the movement of dark forms within, we rushed over the brow of rock-falls and cascades, stumbling towards the black opening and the monstrous resonances - the movement of great weights and again a low incantation. We ran fearfully into the dark haven. All sounds now welcomed us.

The shapes moved once again. As we approached the cave mouth, purple drapery shifted in the dark recesses and the glint, now and then, of exposed metal was seen.

Sassafras! Save us!

We plunged into the cave.

CHAPTER FIVE

The shape of the teacher blocked the mouth of the cave. The long cloak reached down to the ground and obscured his shape but, in the small light, the grey face and darkened eyes looked straight forward, clearly, and other eyes gazed beyond us to the valley outside and this fearful light.

Sassafras did not flinch. He beckoned his followers to move further into the cave. There they moved in the very dark recesses and the light from their few lamps picked out all metal impediments. The sound of the movement of heavy loads broke the air. In a flurry we could make out certain disguised and hideous shapes. These brief glimpses were caught in the moment before cloaks were pulled closely round distorted forms. In the end, eyes alone could be seen and for some of the figures not even these could be made out distinctly.

Yet further to the back there was the glint of machinery and round these objects the figures huddled, trembling, whenever our eyes lit upon one of their structures. The figures were marked as the teacher's helpers: Wisdom said clearly and Friend rapidly agreed that here must be some of the builders of the tower for they gestured the despair we felt at the sight of its twisting, broken wooden stair.

All of this shone in Sassafras' eyes too for we had been told he was beset by nightmare, by failures and dark visions. Close to, the villagers' warnings were seen as incomplete. Sassafras' trials and the anguish of his years marked his shape and what could be seen of his face.

In the back of the cave, darkened structures now became visible and the scene of yet another of the teacher's endeavours emerged as eyes grew accustomed to darker greens and the purple of the cave depths. Bronze caskets covered the furthest reach and in the very back they were open. The figures of those who worked on them were picked out by the flickering of candles which guttered at times in draughts from the back of the cave. From there, another light could be seen - green and rising from the cave floor - an iridescent patch which lit the cave roof. A gentle breeze could be felt. This sweet air was heavy with delicate aromas and from the well of light could be heard slight movement too.

With iron beams the huge chests were lifted from the ground. They first slid till counterweights moved them more and they swung into the air, helped by Sassafras' workers who, shielding their faces turned rapidly away from our gaze and kept their hooded faces turned away from the reflection of the whirling image outside.

The light now caused the sides of the caskets to take on sparkling colours and the rays spun from the sides and reflected on pools of water on the cave floor. This light then moved to speckle the cave walls, flying over the roof and darting between large hanging rock forms - and between frightened faces.

Sassafras gestured speed and the workers adjusted their beams over more and more metal chests. We stood amazed. Such great weights were then moved quickly toward the back, and at the back yet more were lowered gently into the luminous pool. Now the light welled up and the glowing fluid ran about the workers' feet. It caught in their clothes so that the fear in their eyes at the strange light overwhelmed them: they turned repeatedly, gesturing entreaties to their leader and so indicating each of these accumulated misfortunes.

Sassafras clearly was able to protect all wandering souls: wordlessly he gestured that his vision offered more than this whirling image ever threatened. For greater dangers than cracks in the earth - and that which caused the village now to smoulder beneath us - had beset the lord of misfortune in many years.

Wordlessly we agreed that the dreamer was here to help and to guide. Wisdom stepped forward and pointed fearfully at a night sky lit like day and at the twisting night cloud; at rays stabbing down and at the unnatural violet of the glow from above. Trees and grass, we could see, were shrivelling in its light.

As if there could be only one question we spoke or we gestured forcefully:

"Sassafras, teacher, what is that?"

But other than to describe this fearsome beauty there was no explanation Sassafras would give. No reply that might show even partially what forces now collided.

Sassafras' hand, raised up, showed that about us moved great dangers and that he as guide might save us from all such threats. Willingly, Sassafras would show us that which might endure. Only this way might we then understand the threat and these fearsome currents in the night.

And there was much to satisfy us in this reply for we hoped for assurance. The teacher examined each one of us as he spoke, but words came so slowly that it was the face, eyes and gestures which impressed his presence upon us. Not one of us came closer than the wildest of these gestures might allow and the workers, too, avoided contact. They avoided as well

Sassafras' deep eyes and even the position on the ground directly in front of him.

Sassafras, the custodian of this dream, held our trust. Willingly we acquiesced. Sassafras could lead us from now on.

He gestured about him. Huddling at the back, the workers, the strange and twisted figures, continued their tasks and so moved the last chests to the back of the cave. There they raised them slightly and then lowered them speedily into the luminous pool. Some were heavy, others empty of great weight contained instead fluid like that glowing foetidly to great depth at their feet.

By a corner at the back we gathered. The last chest was now visible through the green surface. We waited, still distant from the hooded forms who neither spoke nor remarked our presence except in fearful gestures and with vain efforts at concealment. We waited hopefully in this way for Sassafras' command.

The teacher limped forward. The strange lights on the cave roof caught now and then at the drips of water and the rock fingers reaching down from the roof. These forms descended to just above Sassafras' head and sparkled there. Sometimes they shone in the colours of the pool, at others in the violet from the cave mouth.

In the very dim recesses workers, cowering, set light to torches and, carrying them ahead, illuminated what could not be seen before: the darkened opening behind a small prominence. This gave the workers much relief and caused us to think of passageways in rock and the remains of animal life; of dark chambers, silent currents and the flow of air and water.

We followed Sassafras' shape. It was difficult to see this form as anything but beloved; difficult to look into Sassafras' eyes and not feel the strength of wisdom and concern. This great healer was himself scarred with the wounds of his many misfortunes: as he walked, the effect of some mechanical device could be seen for he faltered between one step and the next and was only propelled forward by some unseen force, some device which his long garments concealed and which allowed him to walk. It allowed him especially to accommodate the unevenness of the cave floor. Stopping before the dark entrance at last he turned and before he spoke, began his gestures: rehearsing before us the sense of what he would say. He raised us therefore to joyful heights with just the anticipation of his words. Everything which surrounded the teacher made this moment delightful, of matchless faith; a pure celebration.

Such love overcomes all doubts. The sound of the destruction outside, the former failures of this teacher, even the fact that he was not now whole; nothing could change our regard for the dreamer. It spread before him, it dallied only long enough to gain certain helpers' strength - then to pass on among the others, so growing and growing. Helplessly, willingly, we tumbled and sank deeper. In this way it changed the shades in the cave. Quite in order now were the natural hostilities - the strike of blinding fire from above, a broken tower, the loss of our comrades; burning air, searing violet light. Suffering was now all one and danger too: the whirling image and the cracked earth beneath.

Sassafras was keen to bring us together. Even though we were able to approach only with the greatest difficulty it was necessary to gather all courage together, to brave his gentle presence and to listen closely to what he would say.

On a short journey into the earth, he said, we would uncover secrets close to the heart of the endeavour.

The workers became excited. They rushed to and fro always keeping their eyes turned from Sassafras' face but, nevertheless, in their rapid pacing they swept nearer to the teacher on every pass. They swept past us in turn: they grabbed and clutched at us so that we too danced, though distant from the gesturing grotesques. We danced away the terror outside, the memory of the plague swamps and a hundred other perils; and too the figure of the Pursuer striding through banks of mist and crossing from one promontory to another, breaking trees as he progressed, pulling at boulders and disturbing rocky cliffs by the march of his feet and the sound of his cries.

Sassafras' gestures became larger still - his unseen mechanisms clicking and whirring beneath his garments - and he indicated that a larger part of all his work was to be seen beyond the dark entrance, that until we could have sight of these wonders, fear was out of place and concern for any lives still in the thrall of the evolving glistening universe outside was to be discounted; certainly not our proper concern.

Gladly we obeyed. To a low humming the helpers moved towards the entrance. With their torches high they moved through vaulted space amid the pendants of rocks and the dripping water. They passed the glowing pool and glinting caskets and their light fell on speckled rock surfaces and at droplets forming. Low mist at times clouded the air. The workers' voices now rose in the air, they held the lord of misfortune's name highest of all and they chanted joyfully:

"Sassafras!" And the cave echoed.

"Gift of the starless night!"

"Sassafras, seat of aspiration, lord of little!"

And the torch-lit procession moved on. Encouraged by those jerks by which the leader moved, we followed the cries of the workers, not yet able to join in their praise but gesturing deference to the steely eyes, the unmoving mouth and the grey gaze of our teacher. We moved into the dark entrance.

Over an uneven floor, at times gravelly, at times deep in water, the whole procession moved. The air became clouded with smoke from so many torches and the flames licked at the hanging rocks above, the finger projections; and sent shafts of light into crevices above our heads. These holes stretched downward from greater heights and the light from these flickering flares penetrated there only partly, for the passageways twisted: there was no view to the dark upper reaches. Down some, echoing draughts descended: from others water poured and dripped.

The passage became narrower. The company now had come together: the workers, cowering away from us, and we, horrified at such close contact with these distorted forms. The water became a torrent, it carried us on. To the noise of tumbling water were added other sounds not yet discernible - sounds heard above the sighing, above the echo of footsteps on gravel and the rush of water at our feet. At times these droned, at others they caused great vibrations to rack the passage walls.

Sassafras showed signs of impatience: his voice was raised to quieten the fears of our companions.

The icy torrent swirled round our legs and cut paths between us. It rolled gravel and small rocks with it. At times it caused feet to stumble, the water then would carry off a traveller or a worker into the dark region ahead. They floated this way faster and faster so that they were swept from our view and their cries became added to the echoing rhythms ahead.

The passage turned round a larger boulder. The light from torches picked at shining streaks in this rock: green and gold whorls and the reflection of sparkling white. The streaks passed upward from one edge and sloped into the roof.

We slid past it with awe. Sassafras too, as if confronting some talisman, touched its beautiful veins and ran grey fingers where they overlapped as if this was to mark some future direction.

Past the jewel rock and in the light of our torches we saw the torrent suddenly break and tumble over rocks into an enormous cavern. The cool air was filled with the flight of a thousand insects. In the glow that surrounded us we were transformed.

All about was blue. As the last worker floated down the cascade we looked about us. Everywhere, the glint of blue reflected from the wings of insects and the crystal hues of the rock above. In the cold of the vast opening our breath clouded, mingled with spray droplets and so glinted in red, at times in purple, most often in blue. From where we stood, wet and breathless, we looked down to a cataract without end, to water plunging into mist, into blue spray. Rainbow hues.

Above our heads light shone out. Projections from the roof descended through the haze. Columns reached down to where the floor of a great abyss might be. Were the air clear, vistas between humped island rocks and the swirl of water pools would be seen. The confluence of streams and whirlpools lay far below our feet.

In the rock face small openings were visible. To these other pathways led, and within, figures and large shapes appeared. But near to the centre of this great space and above the blue mists was a table-rock where, behind straight columns like pillars and glinting now and then whenever the light from above cleared and its movement became visible, was the bright metal sheen of a giant wheel.

This wheel turned. Cranks rose and fell as the wheel rotated. Above hissing steam pipes and shafts; above dulled metal shapes connected by vast piping; above slowly vibrating chambers this huge wheel turned. It was as high as Sassafras' tower. It moved slowly flashing now and then in the light from the bright channels above. In clouds the insects swirled, they illuminated bright metal as they flew.

We stood there amazed. Straight away Sassafras' helpers moved on. And now as they approached the nearest entrance they made their first sounds: they picked their awkward passage through the larger boulders, they hissed, they gestured. Mainly their movements indicated parts of the machine. Their hissing, certain hard clicks of the tongue and the jerking of arms and even lower limbs formed some base speech. Thus they prepared a way for the teacher and they helped those figures partly seen in entrances; those gesturing and some standing still on the gantries around the table-rock and its machine.

Sassafras climbed steep paths which fell away on both sides. These paths crossed and joined, they followed ridges - the only ground visible above a shifting sea of insects and blue light; and Sassafras' cloak set the light-flies into eddies as he moved. He reached the table-rock and climbed to the top.

At the height of the gantry where a stone tower was hewn from a single prominence, he turned and gestured that we should come.

We approached Sassafras, his arms and his face now jerking spasmodically. We looked in wonder at the construction below him - of glass and steel, formed with giant cylinders and with pipes stretching away into the cavern walls. Sassafras' machine clearly reached as far as any of us could see.

He indicated our place to stand and he motioned about him, making it very clear that in a short space of time he would begin to speak.

CHAPTER SIX

Sassafras gestured a digging motion. "Many years ago I was present at a great transformation.

"In my life the first work that I was able to do was moving earth from a pit-digger's path. Just a few of us worked closely with the Digger, nevertheless, only rarely did I glimpse the man at all during that early period, the period when his efforts grew daily. At times the sleeve of his garment might be noticed or muffled instructions to another worker might be heard, but for the most part our sight was obscured by the earth wall and the shadow within the pit. Later heavy linens shielded the view.

"The earth piled higher, the Digger never stopped. At night we would gather round fires and contemplate the glow from the Digger's pit. We would watch the earth mound too as it grew in the dark. On these occasions, workers with wooden lifters, carts and chutes moved about silently, their paths illuminated by flares and the light from camp fires.

"Lit by a glow lasting every night, digging devices and many more of unknown purpose were built and settlements were founded. By our fires stories were told of the great work that we undertook. These stories caused great rumours, opinions and movements to spread.

"As the settlements enlarged, the work of these helpers grew so that the yellow glow spread outward and those close to this vision became dazzled by its light. These figures walked with eyes cast down and with their own helpers to guide them - such were the demands of work close to the Pit Digger's special illumination.

"These close workers were protected from the attentions of others. For these others would seek the close workers out to press them endlessly for hints about the Pit Digger's gigantic task. They would gather about them closely. They would importune them with promises and clutch at their clothes to hold them back if one such golden being should stop in this way to discuss the work of the man of light. I myself had long ago been separated from the Digger's side, for as his needs had grown, more powerful helpers appeared at the most appropriate times.

"And now at night we were entertained by tales of the Pit Digger and his work. Bands of wandering zealots visited us gathering stories of our work and delighting us with descriptions of rare visions elsewhere. The work for all of us was beyond understanding. Only by the tales of these wanderers was it made even partially clear. In the night we would delight in their stories, sing with them of the great workings of our companions. And it was a certain joy to think of the Pit Digger's fine work, for his shining light spread by night to touch even the mountain tops and sprang, we felt, from some deeper will. We saw great things would come from an illuminator such as he.

"It thus became necessary to study the sayings of the close workers - so that I began my later tasks only on the periphery of the adventure. Certainly there had been nothing simple about my work but it was possible to discover certain underlying intentions in the form of the network through the earth; the generation of the light and the reason for its affinity to starlight, to the silhouettes now present on the nearby mountain tops - and the fact that no strange influence now fell on the valley.

"These rare individuals made time precious indeed. Their own helpers are known to restrain them forcibly whenever food has to be pushed into them or their frail bodies are tied down in order to rest. Their discussions then take place without end.

"I have been able to speak with such unusual individuals and their illumination has filled my days gently. These great workers had planned the growing tasks of the settlements and now directed our efforts. I felt that, throughout, my particular talent had been noted by our leader, I was thus unusually required to work within my imagination and to give all my trust to this illumination and to the worker underground. My talent shone in adversity.

"When finally on the perimeter itself, no longer the carrier, hewer, the craftsman in wood, I responded to all hostility. I made the outer regions secure and guided those who entered our adventure: I was the first such helper: a suffering toiler after perfection, an artisan, a seeker, the Pit Digger's helper."

It was clear the teacher knew of our hopes for he made some gestures catching the movement of tides, the path of a river through the centre of a cornfield. We saw him then as many must have seen him: a lord of misfortune. Sassafras continued:

"Other helpers lightened my nights with the great wisdom of their stories. My skills in adversity developed with direction from the leader's helpers. This has made me a tireless seeker too. At the perimeter I met with the hostilities reserved for all of our ambition. And while I also helped the newcomers, the forces that we met took on strange and even devious forms. The death of birds and the decay of trees - fears of the poisoned rain - made each of us watchful on the boundaries and we examined ourselves deeply whenever a new influence was brought to bear, a plan rapidly adopted or a new face accepted by virtue of diligence or natural talent.

"The workers inside the adventure, suffused with the wish which lit the whole sky and under my direction, were able to construct very necessary devices. Moats and wall perimeters were established quickly. When fires in the surrounding forests were lit and great winds arose with the upward rush of heated air, it was my linen shields and wooden deflectors which caused winds to spiral quickly outward, move across the marsh and so expend themselves on all distant obstacles.

"Whenever animals which surrounded us ran wild or suffered from plague or some other madness, the simplest solutions were tried. Nets funnelled the great perils in on themselves, back to areas of the most extreme hostility.

"But among our fellows there was a fear greater than that for the poisoned river and perhaps the death of burrowing life forms. There was the danger which came daily to our walls. On one occasion we heard a lone voice and saw a figure too, one bearing fruit and small captured animals from surrounding hillsides. Most travellers had heard of our exploit and because of great need covered vast distances to our side. Their cries, sounding above the high winds about the perimeter walls, would be of terrible hardships and their own unimaginable concerns.

"In the past, certain of these venturers caused us much damage. The great fire which swept our settlements followed the arrival of one such band - the wooden buildings cracked and broke in the heat; our work throughout stopped. (Though the glow from the pit faltered, it did not give out: the Digger himself thus took no release to ensure his own safety.) The work of the adventure, though, was diverted and so the rise of our aspiration was interrupted. Certain close workers, however, felt the work was quite properly deflected: they selected for themselves less and less critical roles and so often disappeared from our force quite effectively.

"We were concerned about such workers. Through them had come the growth and fine achievement of the adventure and now dissenting ideas might change our efforts and accomplishments in ways not even partly understood.

"The wandering bands of singers - and the glances exchanged with those near to the close workers betrayed our apprehension. Shortly, as a consequence, the perfect safety of our leader was established - his safety and that of his work below the ground.

"These workers thus became a special concern. I have examined the dangers. And the threats that our great exploit has withstood have come from all quarters. The tales that supplicants beyond our walls have told of the perils in forests and in crossing streams have armed me against the dangers attacking our exploit itself.

"Once, on a bright day a group of such travellers approached the central regions. The story they told was of a journey through a lowered walk, a passageway, worked below the earth and open only at the very top to the sun as they moved by day - and the stars and occasionally the moon. Tree creepers, grass and many earth falls made their passage difficult but they had been driven by a particular need. They moved through their sunken way through water which covered their path to such depth that they waded, at times even swam. They progressed through tracts where the growth of vegetation from above covered their path completely. It caused them to brave the thorns and many crawling stems; and poisonous mites among the leaves.

"Towards the end, so accustomed to these dangers, these travellers could see a great many perils above ground. The Pursuer, roaming in the forests and grasslands above, made the air resound with terrible cries. They watched and listened as awesome beings met, contested violently and so swiftly killed one another.

"The journey of these travellers had been terrible indeed. At last, approaching our ramparts their path rose and they would have been forced nearer and nearer the surface. Instead, working only with their hands, they deepened their sunken path; where it would have surfaced altogether, they continued in the same direction and after many seasons came close enough for us to hear.

"We, looking down, could not help but admire their feat. As their digging continued at night, crowds gathered to watch the progress and to encourage their efforts. At once we wondered where such expert earth movers might best be employed in our adventure. As they part-tunnelled their way towards us, we sent out messages to our other workers. I myself, aware of the dangers which they had braved, wanted them to help in combating the attacks on our boundary.

"As they approached, the occasional glimpse of them through the top of their excavation showed shapes twisted by the excesses of their journey.

"At once, horror and a delight of the afflicted ran through the crowd. We called down to them to show themselves fully. They climbed to the surface:

""Praise this day!" We saw broken hopes and their nights burnt by fire.

"Another moved closer. Cowering, they displayed the last desperate resistance of a defeated prey. The spasms of these sufferers caused starts and flickers of recognition to pass swiftly along the rows of workers and at once the story of their flight could be read in gestures, occasional spoken words and mimed entreaties.

"I attended silently to what they tried to say. They gestured: their efforts and those of the great venture had been so similar that their silent communication and our stabbing rays had met and opposed each other violently. (At times they grappled among themselves. They climbed over each other's bodies, occasionally they made deferential gestures upward and between each other.)

"Terrible onslaughts began early in their work and their nights were plagued by attacks. In great fear, encircled by cries - trees shook as a pursuit began among them - the last survivors ran out. They found their sunken path as the cries multiplied so that it was very clear that their flight was the one exceptional action that might then have been contemplated. In their fear there was some beauty and in the cries of those who fell to other beings, a music like that of stars.

"The bright, white heat of this fear shone blindingly before them and there were some who were able to glory in terror, feel a special joy at their very own fear.

"We saw their gestures directing this delight. As they reached upward, standing for the first time on the grass near our walls, they made vertical gestures, moved hands sightlessly over their forms and when some limb or whole body of a supplicant was sensed to tremble most violently, this quivering form was raised higher and higher into our view. The mass thus appeared in certain vibration, and we too saw the ecstasy of fear. Henceforward we might hear the moan of terror that certain recollections evoked. We might then join in the celebration of the desperate, rejoice in the tearing of limbs by giant broken claws.

"Their agony rose clearly before us. And the silent beasts that produced this gentleness were all about us too. In the distance those that pursued these figures now resembled the trees. Silently, the movement of teeth and sucking mouth parts shifted gently with the leaves. As we looked toward these great distances, nothing which appeared familiar remained as it seemed. We saw the chase through grasslands along tracks which crossed and re-crossed. Defenceless life ran before all. Everything living had to die.

"As these travellers were welcomed into our number, as great defences opened wide, the impressions of such destruction faded to spread misgivings into each corner of our adventure: a shimmering image.

"And the alien ideal was a poison within - and attacks, too, now centred upon us. At times the sky darkened with visible signs: flocks of dying birds, insects swarming. When, at deepest night, all lights failed us vast shapes freely moved among us unseen. There was no area of our wishes which was not to suffer.

"Some strange feeling was now disturbing our efforts. When the fire started within, the dispersed new workers were lightly dissuaded from this new direction. By force they had caused a rigid contemplation, an examination and questioning which dulled the light from the Pit Digger's shafts.

"The great exploit was to be blessed with the development of this light. But we were made certain that elsewhere others had completed their efforts. At night the other centres began the long decay to loss of hope. Certainly, during their stay, the glow from the Digger's pit dimmed and the warm winds from his network under the earth no longer blew hotly and we all felt that life with this great leader was dulled to some small degree.

"Our efforts redoubled. New parties were dispatched to the lands beyond the hills where great settlements were formed. And where, too, visits were made to all living in the hills and by the rivers. Their stories of the great danger that we had brought upon ourselves abounded. On the tracks, the remains of victims devoured while still in flight greeted us and stories were told of these victims' secrets while enveloped in folds of skin, while they were held in contracting muscle, and drained of fluids within by raw sucking parts.

"Our leader showed himself alive to just this threat from travellers. For now the great excavation stretched further to all sides than we could imagine. By its means the fears and dreams of these people surrounding us were brought close to hand. We heard these hopes and fears as they whispered them in our echoing passageways. Terror now bound all.

"But helpers existed whose work went beyond the refined wooden structures, the wind vents, chutes and transporting ways, and we saw that our work, so well established now - the model for the dispersed settlements - needed protection greatly; that delicate understanding would be necessary and the collection, too, of separated intelligence. And plans were then made and many workers encouraged in this venture so that they worked all day and night. And their vast hall housed the growing plans and the schemes that were there established. At times in the night, the charts, maps and drawings of devices and greater plans still were discussed so that arguments and the caring concern of all of our followers illuminated these nights. They discussed the larger systems that now protect and develop our leader's great work. At once certain models could be made. Straight away wooden structures of automatic gates emerged. So, too, the refilling wells and the moats with currents, moats with waterfalls and the cascading lights - those lights which might fall promptly from the sky. Our safe world could be beautiful and we worked diligently towards this special aim.

"Swiftly I took up my role. I arranged such needs in quick succession. Attacks were suitably deflected and while these proved our greatest danger I was still able to hold only one small part of the perimeter in my control.

"I called upon our other helpers and greater plans were then established. Those schemes which underlie our entire defence drew comparisons between separated hazards. Clear paths, then, led from efforts against the disease of the falling leaves to greatly repeated small animal attack. At night in the hall as the stars were glimpsed through holes and as close workers told of new plans and the changed direction of the Pit Digger, we forged the schemes between threat and response; between violent action and slow, silent gestures of the great venture; the wonderful rising of the brilliant sun."

We looked about us. Each had been moved by this elevating tale. Beautiful Seeker's gestures were now so increased that he too trembled. The movements he made gestured a towering form rising above fears and these dangers.

This image moved upward and quivered slightly with the teacher's completely fixed gaze. Each slightest movement suggested structures: towers and ramparts - and beneath - tunnels, the massy foundations; the beautiful, intricate world.

And the edifice itself shifted in response. Beautiful Seeker's form moved whenever great force opposed it. As a climbing plant, this towering shape grew over and around obscure forces. When some form of danger - a withering wind which might freeze all fluids - caused growth to stop and life to ebb noisily away, the tendrils and, the towers, too, enclosing those vulnerable areas moved slightly and winds were deflected. Gently they were made to twist, expend their energy in eddies and coldly to embrace Beautiful Seeker's structure.

The teacher saw the Seeker respond to his demands.

The rest looked round still further. At once the vibrations of the Seeker were caught up by the Family who, coming from the ocean, made rapid aquatic movements: they detailed the rise of air through supported weeds, the quick sideways closing of broken claws, the flow of twisting water through runnels and humped island weeds, the cry of seabirds. All these things they made very clear and moved closer, they sweetly moved towards the Seeker's edifice which towered above mists and shuddered too from the roaring ocean.

Sassafras smiled. This image was to become dear. And the night which blew winds through turrets progressed; clear water trickled down broken, sloping walls and, falling then through channels between masonry, rushed on to mingle with spray and blue sea. The light from the sky above the sea and the tower grew stronger.

First Leader, the Victor Over Every Misfortune and Friend joined these gestures and we became swept up in the celebration of the rise of the sun. Beneath the ground burrowing and turning forms moved up towards the light.

Sassafras moved to make a gesture. As we looked about us the mists were clearer and the devices stood silently, vibrating, shifting to the distance: light tunnels, intricate pipework; massy, once gently moving forms. These vistas stretched great distances into the rock.

Light filtered from hanging cave shapes above. Water ran down twisted and massily descending rock fingers - fingers and a landscape of valleys and mountain ridges above our heads. It caught at glistening cylinders and driving rods: about the machine lights turned and changed in hue.

In our dance we gestured acquiescence: such works were a strange pleasure, clearly the subject of Sassafras' dreaming. Our gentle desires focused on the vision of the leader.

And some were able to look into the brilliants. The gesturing and the living structure suggested faceted views like the branched and towering openings to this cave's walls, and the beauty of the idea was then to be seen. We saw the rising light generated deep within the earth, and we saw the rich endeavour of one exceptional creator.

This excitement of the vision; this touched, bright, sparkling connection of powers. The dream from this dance's leader carried us swiftly to Sassafras' fantasy above our heads, the sweet hope above our heads, and the intricate paths. The lights flashed other colours.

Those that we had known changed: green, the colour of sedges and grasses; warm earth passages in the grasslands. Blue, which surrounded the Family on their journey in the ocean and up the torrents of freshwater streams; this changed. And vermilion, grey, the blinding white of lightning attack; black and the scorched brown, blood-red and purple depths: the colours of distant trees, the imagined and fearsomely coloured forms of dangers that now resembled trees; green and bright stars.

Above these dangers, these bright lights, one single colour predominated.

CHAPTER SEVEN

The Beautiful Seeker's gestured tower rose higher. Sassafras guided it so, like his own, it faltered but then rose. Beneath it a valley spread out. Here mist hung low, the Family took to gesturing the fall of the river.

The centre column of a tower rose up and the light paths spread out from it. Around this column, though deep within the earth, and with bright light shining up inside, the small rooms and observatories nestled. The eyes of the helpers there looked into giant systems of lenses. By their means were recorded the secret movements, all expressions and every gesture.

Channels spreading from the base of the tower sent light shafts through cavern walls and into holes and hollows throughout the earth. Along water paths they stretched beneath rivers and through the channels of those underground streams: as brilliant paths, as light reflecting from jewel mirrors and over great distances.

These rays spread through unseen ways and where the earth dipped they might surface, might cut paths through branches of trees, pass unknown through buildings and private dwellings; recording there things seen and unseen. These light channels carried the greatest secrets.

And in the tower where the Seeker gestured highest were the mirrors and illuminated screens, the workers recording each gesture and each expression; those recording too the massing of birds and insects, the underground endeavours of small threatening animals and the accumulation of the débris of streams.

This work had taxed Sassafras for years. And the movement of tides, the soft movement of ripples, the flow of bubbles in streams and between pebbles; these detailed views were now presented to the leader and his helpers. The lord of misfortune had seen the shadows fall across the wide beach at the ocean as each member of the Family rose from protecting rock-pools and the embrace of seawater plants. In this gentle world they had lived warmly, never raising their bodies out of the heated sea and consuming only food washed toward them each day. They lay there all the time on warm fluid beds in the sun.

The comfort of life in these summery wastes preserved and defended them. Only by the expansion of their world were they threatened. Their languor had about it all the success of lower green plants, the motes in the ocean. And they rested flaccidly in these tepid pools, they fed and they lay removed from all dangers. The wind moved them slowly, the waves lapped over their bodies, all else presented only some aspect of uncalled-for danger. As each lukewarm wave approached, their bodies were part lifted in breath, they expired with the wave's gentle movement and fed by its chance transport of good things.

As the sun beat down, nothing could call them to greater action than the slow tidal rocking, for each random desire promised them only less than the caress of small waves, the sun's gentle rays and silent still moments in bright light. The ocean sky was blue, small seabirds flew overhead and dipped.

But other light cut through their pool. Stabbing, rays passed through drifting fronds, reflected themselves from rocks and bubbles at the escape of air from weed beds and in water moving outward to the sea.

Each ray throbbed. It struck across the pools catching at the warmed flank, the slightly heaving chests, beautiful limbs. Each ray moved, it focused on every unusual and involuntary flexion, each slightly opened pore.

With us now, the Family mimed their own arousal, they joined Beautiful Seeker in his dance. The teacher, at first only joyful at the portrayal of some early contact, was soon swept into reverie by the movements indicating the Family's awakened need. All needs: gentle winds, valued communication over small unfulfilled desires (curiosity about the texture of rocks or of the skin; uncertainty about the finer movements of celestial bodies; the excellent hope of communication with trees), these needs caused their great forms to stir slowly, for while rumours and the hope of such a great exploit did exist there remained some slight imbalance; and the knowledge of the Pit Digger's work had spread, spread further still. The joyful members of the Family pursued the Pit Digger's work. They rose from the water.

Caught nakedly by the light, standing above the warmed ocean, light paths stretching from outcrops above their heads, the whole Family were examined by minute rays stabbing from under rocks in headlands. The drift of wind through body hair was examined and, too, the moving lips. Every feeling shifting there was recorded by distant eyes, misshapen eyes, eyes focused on the spheres and lenses, on the light projected onto domed ceilings, eyes in obscured rooms and where the distorted figures of helpers moved. These helpers, too broken now to assist in any way but by signalling, tallying - their disturbed and half-live minds thus bent on single twisted movements - these helpers recorded everything to be seen. On charts they set down each gesture and movement of lips. They detailed the beauty of the Family, the near-content of their gaze and, too, a certain response to the gentle call to the great adventure.

The Family set out happily to find the very centre of the disturbance. Thus the Family was called inland and proceeded via river, stream and lake towards our other meeting.

Never far from the comfort of water where they moved through mud banks of streams - in the reed-bed estuaries and up gently flowing rivers - the sound of their wading, or their movement beneath the water, spread through dense areas of water-fed growth. Here, trees themselves were not able to increase - and the figures moving under the darkest canopy stalked them sightlessly, moved in the heat of noon, attacked fitfully their own bodies and massed insects against them. The light rays, emerging from crystal rocks, now burned paths through the foliage, caused insects to dance superbly, and stealthily followed the Family even where sluggish water formed cataracts.

The smallest gesture in their progress towards our meeting was noted in the tower.

And we could see too that the leader had knowledge of each of our number. The garlands of the grass maidens, the medallions from their nights with the lords of the rocks dazzled this company in the cave as the images were raised by the teacher and by the Family's brave dance among light-flies.

These rays struck out and through the luminous blue haze of insects we became dazzled by the brilliance of talismans. When Friend joined the dance she described nights which such maidens had spent within jewel caves - caves which sparkled in the light of whorls, whorls shining in rock faces and cave walls; translucent, brightly coloured mineral forms. And such forms allowed the sight to penetrate within solid rock itself, made channels of light in the massy walls and shone in all the hues of Sassafras' own dream rock at the cave mouth; of the striations spreading outward and of this tumbling waterfall and blue-tinged light.

Driving and beautifully formed, ghost-edged, and with brightly lit eyes - dark skins - the rock lords were seen faintly in underground broken light. And when they approached, Sermountain, Borage, Bittersweet and the Sedges, all the maidens, seeking only this light from the rocks, rigidity, the warmth of contact; at once gave certain slight cries and descended.

Borage, hope and beauty, was met singly. The odours - sulphurous from the depths and, too, the light air of summer - encircled all. And this dance - the violent play of these lords' vision, the pursuit of wonderful works - caused the tautened network to surround the beautiful dreamer. She sang for all to hear:

"When ice sinks into cracks and passes between rocks, lord above us in the mountains, Fine Will, I have thrilled to touch, have penetrated rich earth. Come, join me."

Ice-water descending slowly from her limbs, Borage moved at first in her haze of ice crystals, by pure will becoming engulfed. The lord reached out.

The winds on mountain tops above all heads circled. Among the crags lit brightly, a rock moved suddenly, touched one larger and their echo sounded.

In the greatest cave hall they danced for the rock lords' dread eyes. Each beautiful form disappeared into shadowed regions and into small tunnels there pursued by one or many of the brilliants; and the white of their garments disappeared into dark passageways and the delight in their gestures became intensely heated too.

In the recesses where colonnades were draped, where arabesques displayed these lords' origins, cries of strangeness rang out. In the heavy air these maidens departed, and so dying remains floated silently past.

Raised pediments led to the central shining figure. This huge shape - dark night birds took flight through remnants of his hair - brought a central light to this great hall: he stood brokenly erect; he was lord of their creation, of desires in disarray.

The Lord of the Rocks, towering above the stone-chequered floor - portions were raised with half-empty light vessels and their veils; with shrouds; with discarded broken armaments of lords seen through pestilential air - was thus some figure of disturbed desire.

And we, dancing, vibrated discordantly. Tremors ran through the turning wheel above Sassafras' head and the unsympathetic changes of the revolving piston, the pace of Beautiful Seeker's dance below sent rhythms through the rock itself. The blue cloud of insects undulated, lapped at other mounds and even engulfed the elevated structures.

We became threatened ourselves. Fearfully, Beautiful Seeker climbed higher. The warm air enclosed him. The Seeker's form, embedded moistly, became carried backward, upward and into night.

The air was supporting for those in the Lord's cave. This supreme figure, limbs rising spasmodically, vibrating with the pleasure of wood-armed lords - the hunting, forced gestures which inspired certain dark pursuits - this figure in his paroxysm gave vent to pleasures, and to fears. We were greatly attracted to this terrible vision.

Unaccustomed changes began: the slight lifting and gentle bending of otherwise hard extremities.

The grass maidens departed. This changing form, now translucent, was becoming dispersed. The timeless Lord was bent backwards. Now many times its natural length, his figure floated above the ground. The Lord's deep, dark eyes stared lividly towards the roof of the chamber as the dismembered lower limbs drifted further, became longer.

The backward twisted body, beating, moved in time with vibrations from crystal paths in the rock - ruby and vivid green crystal forms and the channels of bright images in walls, rocks and crevices. The departing figure reached out to visions deep within walls. These lights pulsed and the damaged, receding exercise of the lords' will faded. These half-dreams ran on - a sweet taste - while the lords of the rock rushed to and fro. They examined their crumbling edifice.

Columns broke and splintered. What remained - the Lord's greater design - now slid down silently. Red and sulphurous lava welled up, it devoured the solid rock, it caused everything above to char: crystals on the pediments, the outlets from light channels, these lords' armour, draperies touching stone. All speedily descended to the moving surface.

And the maidens retreated from this venture and in the grasslands - running small fingers over limbs, silken breasts - dressed their hair with amulets and stone beadwork and with laughing gestures thought slightly of their broken lords.

These, twisted by their power, desire, had made one giant assault on the depths of the rocky earth. The practice of absolute will had caused rocks to break.

Once, the Lord of the Rocks, examining crystal, had caused certain cracks to occur - and not at all by pressure, blows or the concentration of rays from a wintry sun. Others, possessing strange sight, vision at night or the ability to hear movements in the earth that all fear, became greatly attracted. A lord was able to rise freely in the air.

Such absolute will produced powers of single persons. All these lords together turned underground night into day. In many encounters they sought the mastery of similar wills.

All else collapsed, all wishes were fully realized. Great and strange deeds overcame all visions. The chance acquiescence of fates lent surprising help.

Their success increased. Such success and absolute will passed together through many separate stages and the lords rose to challenge the tallest trees above the mists and rain.

Above the high ground, trees grew thickly and the cold wind circled in their treetops, twisted the leaves in rapid gusts and chilled those penetrating there. Heavy rain fell down leaf surfaces.

Final Journey responded to the lords' will. Our dearest helper found rest in such heights. By their will had they attached two natures: traveller and tree. We were able to see the strangely gentle way the lords persevered. Final Journey had been carried through the forest. His cry was joyful as wood penetrated fibrous matter. The call passed through woodlands and the broken land beyond. It called for acquiescence, the sweetness the lords bring.

Sassafras raised his hands. The teacher pointed to the light straining from above. A pyramid of forms had been raised before him. At the top, hands trembled in reflection of leaves. Where the Victor circled in rapid paces, wind passed and the leaves and finger branches moved. Heavy and strutting paces marked the despairing steps of lords.

Sassafras gazed upward to light which filtered, in the midst of darkness, from cavern spaces above. From this upper landscape - descending spires and mountainous prominences, cascades - rays struck downward. As the sun's shafts stab out from clouds, light touched rocks and the sea of light flies.

Cascades cut through the rays. Rainbows reflected in the upper valleys. The gesturing pyramid vibrated to one other concern: strange, the Victor motioned, that the cavern is seen to be illuminated, strange that our eyes only now see this light above. So one idea passed speedily from mouth to mouth, and in gestures passed silently among all the attendants of the machine. Each traveller, awaiting Sassafras' dream, recalled his story of the greatest worker and of the wonderful tasks that he had achieved. Between us passed recollections of terrible events: the whirling bright image and burning rays, sulphurous depths to which villagers and the metal structures descended;

the searing of living trees.

Sassafras, gesturing to the radiance above, made desperate movements - but still this moment of the greatest contrast eluded us. The light grew brighter - we raised our arms to greet the illumination, bright as day, and now our silhouettes stretched far over rocks and the airborne sea.

"Sassafras! Gift of the starless night!"

"Sassafras, save us!"

"Blind, under the earth, far from the death of birds and the rise of the sun over cornfields. Blind!"

"Sassafras! Blind, we approached the Pit Digger's work unknowingly."

Beautiful Seeker, the leader of our dance - who had raised the memory of these rivals to the Great Excavator - Beautiful Seeker fell prostrate.

He moved flattened palms over the surface of rock-pools. Beautiful Seeker now showed images of the twisted structures of water-floating life, bulbous and with scaly legs spread wide, so that we all might take on such forms. He drew the beautiful distinction between lords of the rocks - and the one, true and magnificent Great Excavator himself.

What other fine essences met, became filtered and so passed through our own image to then move on as late and broken records of our inadequacy? The noise of the dreamer's machine rising higher was not able to conceal other great movements, the strange passage of bodies in air. The drone from above now penetrated us momentarily as had such echoes in the descending waterway by the jewelled rock.

Metal workers and villagers, the grass maidens and the lost travellers in the cataract; Sassafras' distant helpers and those figures pursued and pursuing - such disturbed dreams of creatures broke beneath the evolving dark cloud. Prostrate, we now dared to look only if the dreamer indicated our safety. In this way, we were able to witness chains of other helpers - files

60

of broken figures weighed down by burdens. They were the twisted forms, victims, revived and defeated figures stretching in lines from openings of other passageways. They moved haltingly, some carried metal parts structured and angled as additions to ventures of the teacher. They themselves expressed such attentions for they glinted and their bodies shrieked, whined and moved in rapid mechanical jerks.

These helpers carried metal chests. From openings in the distant rock walls they passed through the insect clouds and, while still moving, assembled the metal parts. Others they carried with the chests which they escorted closely; delicately moving these great weights over humped island rocks and amid the disturbed light of the bright insects. They filled chests from large vessels - the containers from which luminous fluid was seen to flow - and they carried them very high, they grouped around these burdens closely, they ensured their great safety. At times some helper carried on top of one such chest was able to direct his fellows to avoid certain obstacles, he might then ensure the chest's overfilling. Such numbers, grouped on top of these caskets, caused the greatest difficulties for the carriers below amid swirling light flies.

And at once such impediments, familiar from the cave above the village and, too, from Sassafras' tower, reminded us of the burning light and the savage strike; Sassafras' burning tower. We trembled. Injuries to legs and bodies, cuts to the head and blood from arms, torn hands and fingers - wounds stood out; and dear faces of Final Journey, Fair Union and those carried before us in this cave's torrent caused weeping. We thought of the tower, conduits of light, the teacher's greatest efforts. Channelled light passed among us.

From the tower these rays had struck out: from finely focused mirrors, shining lenses sparkling between one fine curved pathway and the next; from observing lenses and recording plates and into the earth. The light shone along passageways in the rock and caused brilliants on the river's bed. This light passed between gravels. So that every moment was in this way known to the teacher or to his helpers. Gladly we acknowledged that our first steps, perhaps guided by the dreamer, had been directed towards this single exploit, and directed too were the lives of others passed on misty days by the foot of tall cliffs; and in crevices and near sheltered rock-pools, at forest clearings and where rocks outcrop high above the sea.

And our lives were illuminated: sweet, crystal paths to each corner of the dream. The marking by intricate metal machinery - those devices visible through the broken sides of Sassafras' tower - recorded the movements during past travels; the gestures of those unable to help or accompany us and the thousands of other souls whom we no longer contact or never have met. And the light played into the sparkling heart of such devices: the gently moving writing machines, so that in response to such shifts of fortune, rotating cams and the stored weights and shifting levels of Sassafras' mechanical memory responded. They moved, vibrated, turned and thus identified by slight shifts in their levels each movement and the history and fine intentions of travellers.

The strange forms installed in Sassafras' tower resembled instruments in the village metal foundry and those before us in the cave. Momentarily, in the service of the dreamer they could be remembered and the tower was thus the focus of all converging rays from crystalline paths. And the helpers, blinded by such light - the fine, white rays which rose from light vessels and sparkled then down light tubes and down through all the densely packed floors of the tower to disappear at last into the rocks beneath - only at times did the helpers turn from their delicate task of supervising such machines. They turned to look out upon the view of travellers below and to arrange the first reparation and renovation made necessary now by this last, fearsome, fiery lightning strike.

Beneath these rocks, only at times were the sparkling paths partly visible. Through shallow gravels caught up in the wind - those eddies which, moving small stones, displayed the light-filled earth beneath - through rocks and the soil, the great work of illumination beneath the mountains is thus pursued. And the wind and the rain at times disclose this inner secret so that small movements of leaves in circling winds; running water - each expose unexpected bright sparkling points: light shining in these small places and small brilliants from beneath the forest floor. In the darkest of hollows the earth is uncertain.

The rocks and the passage of water are unsure and we have penetrated just some small way when we examine such brilliant points of light.

"Sassafras! There is brightness at the earth's heart!"

The droning, heard on our flight to the cave, grew loud. Large as our present echoing space, the sound of this trembling drew us toward the wind turning, raising fire points and the brightness of embers - and the heat which now penetrates between smaller caves and the rock's fissures. The heated wind circles and touching the rock surfaces flies between greyed ashes in small projections. Beneath these the rock embers glow, raised to whiteness.

What these leave are green whorls and bright, translucent colours which stand out from rock surfaces as striations, blades, the vanes and fins of animal forms; curling layers. What remains of rock spaces is thus burnt away so that any original extent of a jewel rock would be marked by outermost edges of undulating vanes. The wind now circles at great distance from its original path. Red light glowing is thus seen through each layer in turn.

And this is just part of the work of the master. We poor figures tremble at its twists and turns. The shafts from great spaces penetrate the caverns, hanging rock forms, crevasses -

and these rays strike at motes in the air, penetrating finally even deepest clouds. Shadows and hollows spread above our heads.

Rock splinters and slowly shudders as first one rock column and then a fissure crumble in inner heat.

Red and yellow speckles cover the broken surfaces of rocks. The eye is able to see some little way into them as light shines from within. Inside these cells, in small chambers, dark forms move. And there are paths within the rock and at times light descends through these channels, glints on hard surfaces of rounded, quivering bodies - jointed, not different from the crystals themselves but giving bright colours whenever they are able to move an iridescent surface. The crystals break away.

Rock, fracturing and crumbling, falls from between these passages so that the transparent web, remaining some little time after molten rock piles in onto the cavern floor, finally falls too amid burnt remains of light flies' wings.

The cavern wall breaks. At once winds, heated and with faint odours, rush in. The flies become dashed against walls and the glinting metal structures, the light-pipes. Now from these walls golden light - no longer filtered through upper landscapes and the haze of blue insects' wings - this light stabs forward. Horizontal and blinding, the rays illuminate all points in their path, they catch at brilliants, at raised and knotty hands on the table rocks; limbs of workers in procession; caskets - now arrived at the rocky outcrops - and the violently turning machine. Above us, caught in this new brilliant light, the wheel pauses whenever the broken helpers slide dark contents from the chests and move delicately lit fluid into chutes and silvered pathways.

These broken helpers, blinded, shielding faces and twisted limbs from the light, hide where best they can - in rock archways, in the extended shadows from the machine - and so they climb higher, one above the other: they mirror Beautiful Seeker's dance, the silent movement of all travellers. Now we are able to see that the dreamer had one more cause to observe our gestures fully: to pursue movements from the sea, and mountains - and to know what was gleaned from other lords.

Everything had to be observed in this way and now the recording by such helpers bore fruit: thus their rigid structures trembled, they vibrated the greater episodes, and at once we looked down to dark and turning depths, purple, mist-shrouded; the blackened abyss from which these figures of dreams issued - and wind and echoing cries too. These depths lay beneath all that we could have known: dark home to descending forms; echoing, crying. We turned our eyes upward to the bright light at the cave wall.

We looked inside. The wall crumbled and the inner vision became clearer, we were able to look into this structure directly, into the pattern of the work of this Great Excavator. And the Pit Digger's work was many-channelled and filled with bright rays; where the wall had stood there now appeared the honeycombed passages, one upon the other, twisting, entering, turning; broken by vistas of other giant passageways, halls and stairways, crystal engines too.

Even the warmed wind from the passageways raised images so that eyes staring into the bright depths, glancing between high-points of glowing light and surfaces iridescent in yellows and golds, seemed at first to see one set of passages and stairs, then another balcony. And another scene might take their place so that in no way could the wind's images be separated from our gaze. And what we brought to this bright glowing opening could be known to the teacher, might express fears and our joy. Some clearly saw the breaking rock wall and the incandescent interior, wind-etched corridors and the glowing halls. Others trembled at the sight so that their response, the individual fears generated, the joy and the hopes that such vision might produce - these fears blocked and modified their sight. Instead it was the depths from which these helpers of our fine teacher had emerged, the continuing abyss, which these figures contemplated. As we moved forward brilliant and turning stars glinted at us from the entranceway, they cascaded off the rock.

Friend and First Leader, clutching at each other, became transfixed as though contemplating for the first time the small glowing life in damp crevices of trees, the drops of rainwater and strong persons' blood. These forms, so intricate and momentarily beautiful, could capture the close fleeting attention of others' shining eyes. We looked on. With gaze flickering to left and right; small gestures between them of delight, wonder and horror; they might move first close to the brilliant vision, then, taking hold of some slight and interesting bright light between extended arms, they might then dance their fine feelings and their fascination.

Later, these strong emotions would ripple outwards affecting us all and each could only glory in the details of such a minute vision.

Thus the scurrying shapes pursuing and pursued would run glistening between larger green masses - and small legs would be all that could be seen at times protruding from burrows. And the terrible fates that befell certain such beings, the anguished colours flashing between eyes - scaly protuberances - sent cries pityingly between the other travellers and Sassafras' helpers themselves.

And this life, extinguished at times, otherwise changing rapidly, increasing, reached out to fine chords and where we could see beauty we were able to feel fear, final primitive agony and joys of repletion. The world met us vividly.

First Leader was able to see further. In such giant interstices, where huge droplets clung to fine hairs, where they were breathed out of tubules or coalesced under the action of heat or gentle drying; yet smaller forms recoiled. Glistening, rotating, the colours interfering in fine hairs - living jellies moving in vesicles - in the ebb of inner fluids, these reforming, working parts of such small carnivores joined and sucked. And other animals came vividly to mind - those which disturbed the night and followed the death of birds. In darkness figures roamed - pursuing, increased by the rain of blood. Darkened figures were recalled by such bright travellers and Perception and Hope trembled within the ripples. Such visions, they said, must follow all.

Hope wished for the fate of many beautiful life forms. Twisting and displaying all the iridescent openings, the moving fine hairs of flailing swimmers, she was able to give out the dying bright colours, the racing images of a clouding mind. Such union with predators was, she said, greatly to be desired and such a fine outcome might await our entry into the gentle, light, golden region of our leader's leader. Dream of the dream: the finest hope that Sassafras, the teacher, had allowed us to feel.

We trembled at the thought.

Perception showed that this sweetness derived from her. Finely, Perception, the broken and wounded, Perception and First Leader: guides to all other regions, had seen the work of the teacher, our journey, strange life and work in the village - the glistening, evolving image and such lower regions yet to be penetrated. Perception and First Leader moving slowly together broke free from the travellers, moved through light flies, the mists, and disappeared towards the light. They moved, perhaps, towards an entrance.

This was terrible and exciting. Both this minute world and the darkness of the Leader's helpers might be approached.

And now some of us cried out in fear. No entry into the region of a bright beauty - but instead we cried that these friends now moved darkly to the cold depths of the teacher's helpers. And columnar pits disappeared into solid dark rock so that neither the bottoms of the shafts nor even the far walls of such great abysses were to be seen at the end of our shimmering plain. And the wind was not warmed, delicately odoured: howling through minor passageways it rose and carried with it the dust and broken rock pieces from icy lower regions. Glinting, at times these collided with walls in their upward flight, they shattered and so bounced higher, they caused other pieces to join in their ascent and these collided too with certain small patches of colour - greys and browns - clinging closely to ledges, at times moving higher and higher. Observing these, we shuddered as many, holding closely to the rock face, became dislodged by collisions and floated in upward-rushing air - these gesturing above such a great depth and indicating despair if ever their flight should become a rapid descent. Many such figures disappeared from view.

But at the top, some deep-livers did survive and they floated over the brim while the shattered rocks, coming from even greater depths, flew in huge arcs through the air. The rocks rained onto small figures below and those darkened figures from the abyss who managed to grasp some handhold on the fractured rocks at the edge of the wind-blown crevasse - all the damaged figures able to do so covered their faces fearfully, made gestures to conceal twisted, broken limbs and the glint of metal, and scrambled amid the roar and droning of such terrible winds to seek out the safety of rock crevices. They looked for caves, the damp and concealed areas where they might cause their limbs to work once more, where they might try out those parts not wholly theirs and, even then, conceal their presence indefinitely.

The cries of their fellows rent the air. Below, in tunnels and in water courses figures moved. Where passageways wound their way to the edge of these precipices - below were worm-like structures; the deepest areas without hope of light, the gentle winds of summer and - too - the death of birds. Such regions extended to where life might begin; to where the flux of water, icy air and the turning, flowing earth might develop.

68

Growth occurred in small cavities, rocks and in bubbles, in fluids mixing. Black life sprang forth. The unfavoured shapes took on browned and darkened colours. Small life dividing and joining produced fears.

Deep livers were among abandoned life so that when disasters settled in hosts all then rose higher, moved through widening passageways and entered one form of light. The deep-livers walked great distances.

Running before the fall of earth in tunnels and the floods which extinguished all life, they had grown slowly to anticipate and thus to control. For without remedy all fell to the dangers - to the tremors; to rabid, smaller, less fortunate forms still remaining in small cocoons, floating in waterways and infecting the air. All dwellers repelled each other.

The misfortune increased with their efforts. They spread about them the influences of twisted, unpleasant forms. This necessary decay ran down small columns as their breathing echoed: as short sighs, cries of petulance, the recurring demands of empty wastes. These fell too on the ears of more fortunate forms - who immediately turned away - their deaths being assured by such mutual unconcern. Unpleasant beings found their natures brilliantly represented by the sharp glint of broken flints in passage walls, in the ooze from ice-fringed gullies - and in certain dead animal remains.

But by such dull visions were deep-livers able to modify and repair even their own disturbed forms. And the stone increases, the new extra limbs from dried and decaying remains of their fellows - such as these enabled the dark ones to meet many such threats. (These might be made to them in response to disturbed and lowly desires: expediency and the controlled contemplation of the death of friends.) These forms thus began to prosper.

Just then Sassafras cried out. His suffering was of the caring and wounded mentor, the rarest, sweet communicant, the guide and helpmate of all such disturbed souls. He cried out in anguish for this infrequent departure from the work of the Pit Digger; for the rivalling life of the smallest of insects; for the flowing of moulds; for the captives held by oozes and slimes. Sassafras, begetter of nightmare, cried out his torment and his tears fell. They sparkled. For Perception and First Leader Sassafras wept out loud.

This first frailty of the teacher shocked the travellers. Sassafras' hooded shape moved in grief. And these helpers, dwellers, trembled to his sighs. The ascending figures - the wind raised their little hair, they turned and twisted in the updraught - these figures bled and their dismembered forms broke on overhanging rocks. These forms became transfixed on icicles and at times amid ice tendrils; on elongated rocky fingers. They hung with other remains, those identified as long dead creatures, sometimes resembling all helpers but distorted and now decayed so that from the elements of rocks, ooze and the small burrowing forms, shapes and structures developed. They progressed to the broken forms of helpers so that down through any shaft a vision of despairing decay and anguish might remind the teacher, Sassafras, gift of the starless night, begetter of nightmare, that here was the lower life from which perhaps other exploits might grow.

The figures in the shafts cried out in their agony. At the tops, scrambling, raising arms and all other limbs, they gathered about large rocks, they hid from light and they avoided, too, all contact with each other. Rarely they met and at times gave small assistance to some fellow caught between the upward rush of air and rocks and the downward flight to greater depths. Not even the darkest helper now grouped with the leader showed signs of being able to raise such black images: we saw completely the harsh toll applied for all assistance, the rise of certain individuals and equally, too, the way that often strong and elevated forms might then be struck down in their union with others or during the enjoyment of certain discords.

And there was no love and no other lightened feeling in any contacts. The figures only affirmed their first-formed life: of the junction of rocky matter with fluids; broken, disturbed. These dwellers were able to grow with their encounters, with suffering and the rise of original power. In horrible steps their influence, one among others, increased, and at times the dark sun spread its rays inwards.

Sassafras met certain of them. Such meetings, cast beneath a darkened star, gave us all an end to hope. This outcome was greatly to be desired: so extreme a measure so quickly achieved.

At once, the meeting between these earth-forms and the teacher, causing him so much grief, became a certain wonderful pain and therefore useful. At times and only when thus threatened, a fear caused our leader to care. His tears, reflecting light from torrents that brought us to this spot while shining - these tears also took on colours. They produced one hue: green.

Green. Green and glowing as circles of liquid and the burdens that such helpers might carry. Green, which is the colour of solid forms trapped beautifully - as striations. Such rocky practices which flowing lines might suggest cause us nausea and a blinded fear.

Sassafras was allied to these broken figures. He made all aware of regions he had seen. And at an instant the work of this helper became evident to the one exceptional excavator. Through dangers and the pain - crying for help and destroying all helpers - these deep-livers had joined him. And the fear of others in the rocks; strange animal life and, too, the overpowering will - such compulsion was seen to turn all in its neighbourhood.

The lords, beautiful figures blessed by the sun in regions above, these powers turned all to their good and at once others

71

lived in the hope of their acceptance; living becoming sweetly recognized. (All others then had to depart, bleed internally, and in great deficiency expire rapidly.) There was thus nothing that other lives might achieve so acceptably as their own swift descent to death. All others gave such gifts willingly.

But there were fears and hopes other creatures knew well. The mysteries: the brief delight in the touch of cold water, the clear sound and odour of down-rushing fresh air, droplets and bright daylight under the earth that others knew and which there was no way of imagining. Deep-livers, their suppurating limbs and twitching vesicles - there were still transports of light visions which Sassafras might yet show them and which might be turned to greater excess. For at such times it became necessary for those who survived the rise in uprushing winds and passed through branched rising channels to group and cause their own increase - by certain forms of avarice and the comprehension of treachery. They might lighten their own lives with some reverie. They were to delight in the darkness and in their close attention to details of another's agony, they were thus to bring about some part of fulfilment and the darkening of the sun.

Sassafras, broken by their torments, by the vision of their painful birth; reduced to tears by pervading disease - Sassafras, the lord of misfortune, called upon to serve yet fearful of the threats from outside and from sickly birds (these nesting in rafters, open gullies and crevices in rocks might hear words of admiration and die bloodily on the spot) - Sassafras produced a most unexpected union. For our teacher, penetrating intimacies of those hostile to the worthy lord, came silently forward. Sassafras and his helpers thus drew light channels in the most unexpected places.

And the crystal paths ran from depths to protect the Great Excavator; mirrors and prisms reflecting such light round corners. The paths stretched from one observing spot and all

72

activities in the region of the greatest exploit became known and thus recorded. Light paths exposed every detail of the gathering, and the movement of our First Leader. His gestures and invitation were noted by the helpers' fevered eyes. In gallery upon gallery were charted body movements and intentions, the acts and promise of others. Our belief was itself set down and fine essences derived from among our number impressed on our lord and teacher.

"We approach the Pit Digger's side!"

"Wonderful intentions. Happy fortune and misfortune!"

And one spark is directed along light channels. Such contact leaps small gaps and the light, searing, flashes blue as each of the travellers meet: the sharp crack of the brightest light which so sets the eyes blazing, the finer nerves burning, thus extends more. This takes in the seas and the journeys through warm waters, the sun glancing through softened trees and the descent of weakened arms that brush against the hair: the light is now warm to the skin.

Gentle sounds of water surround all. There is now contact with other trees, with mountains - unless some elevated view, sparkling with low sunlight on the small points in rocky surfaces, comes rapidly to mind. This might be warm, and the water rising and the waves flowing might make tender moments with the Family's growing hopes one wonderful series of echoes.

Such points of firm contact: echoes and the memories that make love arise, broken gentlenesses, come before the teacher's gaze. And now the bleeding, pustular forms flow over all such charts. These then claim an absolute knowledge of us. They raise new questions and issue certain directives, they break with all tastes, sweetness.

From the tower, over a wide horizon, the glints where channels might outcrop are seen in blue haze. Through one clearing we catch sight of a cave entrance as eddies turn in on themselves. Such smoke and dust from strangers - the travellers in the lowered walk, the figures on paths that cross and re-cross - even, too, light from leather-clad workers and the sight of metal and heavy machinery - all reaches one recording, is captured in the glow by bleeding eyes and mapped to points on charts and intricately folded plans. These plans are so arranged that variable points might be brought into contact, might possibly move past each other and finally expose themselves in such new configurations that the true meaning of such ordering has required the efforts of hosts of workers to uncover and even now is insufficiently understood.

Sassafras drew himself up and reminded us of his task. Round the tower wind rose. Birds turned round the upper parapets, crying, their own blood rising with them. And beyond these are visions, we are told, of light towers in the distance - and the people move beautifully in broad thoroughfares and the light is seen through them. Consequently in this valley and the next all such brilliants - the channel outcrops and isolated sparkles from water - rise above unaccustomed regions where the sun never shines. And mists lie in all valleys, they then rise up the hillsides and the trees. Caught in occasional bright sunshine they change, sparkle and shimmer.

Sassafras stood above such beauty. Overlooking broken wooden walls, the tower's mosses, earth mounds of insects (these were massing for one more attack on the work of the dreamer), the lord of little maintained all such histories attentively: the lords of the rocks in their retreat in mountains above the grasslands and beneath the earth; the grass maidens in pursuits through crossing paths - and above us too whispers from flying forms and birds deflected by the teacher's angled screens.

And Sassafras saw meetings and junctures in the paths of all figures we might meet: travellers in the depressed paths, others too whom we had passed but never might join - the love of

First Leader, Final Journey's union with trees. The greatest efforts too of the workers of one whole village - their tasks were elaborated by this teacher - and as the dangers besetting the work of the Great Excavator increased, they daily added their involutions and their work became finer; more elegant the turning action of finely honed cams. These devices were developed with such intentions and with their great efforts were original plans, guidelines and words of advice from the teacher increased and broadened, made the subject of the finest response. And now at the point of wonderful entry the work of the Great Excavator came into close contact. We worked our way down intricate paths to these levels and to the work of the Pit Digger himself.

Beneath the earth, this darkness. Nested union, worlds silvered, jutting, folded and evolving, folded rock. And the deep-livers, rock lords, grass maidens, villagers, we travellers and these others across our path - we are not able to speak of them - rare figures, rarer aims too.

Light under the earth.

And the strange colour kept at bay the bleeding death all around. Death of birds.

CHAPTER EIGHT

We entered the cavity.

"This," said Sassafras, "is the territory of the greatest excavator."

In all directions the images tumbled over themselves. We picked our path between the glowing and broken rock crystals from which small life emerged and straightaway followed Perception and First Leader. Such small and penetrating life-forms now were seen by all for, as one looked toward a rock surface or moved the head to some nearer point in the passage entrance, whole vistas shifted and the vision of overhanging water surfaces - their devouring green and bloodied particles, rising leaves in winds - flashed before our eyes. Light filled the passageway, came from hollows and channels and met, focused and coalesced throughout spaces above our heads - in the air, in front of our eyes, even projecting bright images on our bodies and the remains of our clothes. Light covered us all.

And no shadows could form in this light-filled air and in such brilliance no rest for the eyes. What this journey had presented so far - a broken tower and whirling images - merged in such a speedy collapse of time that now identities might be secured:

hope alone, the satisfaction of dreams.

We became distracted as the visions of the Victor and Hope now raced between us and overhead. At our feet could be seen certain views of the base of the tower - so that one rock in the centre of the cavity flickered with the flames from the lightning strike; and the blackened trees all around moved in the slightest wind.

We cried at the burnt vision of our dear dead: Fair Union's place on the ground - and the course of blood running from her wounds. Around our heads the air turned as perhaps the winds circling mountain tops had moved and the teacher pointed to the loneliest stretch of empty air, the passage of clouds and of broken lives of birds.

The cavity led forward. Channels crossed and re-crossed, branched and then divided - to the passages between leaves and under pebbles.

The images passed close to our eyes, heads and bodies. They flashed past as brilliants from the faces of crystals, we saw at first one image within and then another. They passed on. They coalesced, focused more and more and overlapped.

And these visions were available, and our teacher, Sassafras, rushed from side to side. He held his head and controlled the pain of certain disguised helpers outside. We trembled at finding ourselves in such a light passage. We looked forward and back to see perhaps some trace of the greatest illuminator of the earth.

"At points such as this you will not encounter any light from the great worker," said Sassafras, his voice trembling as he controlled his fears.

The guardian of the great exploit, the victim of misgivings, the gift of the starless night, clearly meant that the greatest task now confronted us. His fears were for the beleaguered perimeter, the rise and fall of insect attack and of poison vapours in the sun.

The bright images - from one small crevice near whorls on the rock wall - showed figures dying bravely and water flooding small excavations. Such pain was inflicted that Sassafras, without the help of deep-livers, bore all the anguish for such great endeavour and this pain at once broke his back too. It twisted his form into segments before our eyes so that in steps he revolved this way and that. He was driven by the needs of the great adventure.

We were saddened indeed. Our great lord, by such great weights destroyed - and the cracking of his form sounded in the hollowed spaces and caused such helpers who dared to peer into the entrance to this cavity. The small pieces of which this teacher was made held themselves closely together and at times continued moving. The great gown covered all disjoints and only at times were metal sounds and whirrings to be heard as in the heap at our feet telling movements occurred. On all parts of this gown were projected the images from outside and Sassafras' form, breaking, lost its outline rapidly. We saw little of our parting lord.

As Sassafras tried to speak, noises of disengagement were made: the sound of cloth being torn and metal sliding past smoothed edges, being brought up short by flanges and ridges; and the rustle of hands too, sweeping through garments, clutching perhaps at points of pain.

"This entry is beyond the region that I have been happy to inhabit. My early lessons with the greatest worker have seemed all too clear." Sassafras twitched. We saw, picked out on the sleeve of his gown, the fall of a giant tree, eaten within. We saw insects and spiders moving through its limbs, and saw these leave this space - and weave between blades of grass.

This transition disturbed the lord of misfortune severely indeed.

"What are we to do?" Hope asked and her eyes moved to the Victor Over Every Misfortune - strong, the breaker of bonds, and to Beautiful Seeker, the survivor of the poison swamp. Wisdom, too, took her arm to guide and console. We had in the end to follow all imagined desires. Such central pain was to be guiding and with this object momentary fragments could cause us to understand more - the flash of textures within our view and the vision of timeless, darkened stars.

And the sun would rise over the plain: with winged and turning forms, a once beautiful procession. These separated sights, glimpsed in the clear light between leaves, became more frequent - the strange love of disturbed forms, the new vision of unaccustomed happiness that we need for ever to embrace; and that breadth of change soon to be accomplished.

So the thought of such need sent more pain through travellers' bodies and the call - witnessed by flying forms and the procession in bright sunlight - invited us all.

One figure stood out from the rest clearly. Through swaying, soft-branched trees, along the sunken path leading between closely honed walls and the descending way of the procession, this changing form beckoned all around. It beckoned not in the direction of broken travellers, but toward tall and gaunt trees beyond, wet and shimmering; called between trees and tried to rise spasmodically in the air. All moved nearer by the moment.

We were made bolder by our dying leader on the ground at our feet. Broken by close contact with his lord, he retained only certain motions of digging and the bleak mouthing of words.

Sassafras wanted us to go on. The teacher wished us to leave the light channel into which we had moved, to descend further through the rock, to make the approach denied him and to further his wonderful work.

He motioned the digging that the channel had required, the other branches through rock and the twisting green crystal passages - such lights flashed all around us, in corners and along the convoluted passage. Sassafras was not able to go further and glowing vanes flickered as he indicated one image and then another, all of which proved too much for him, for so great a nature. Sassafras' eyes - and those dark and fearful glances from helpers in the cave space outside - showed their abandonment. The teacher, as before unable to approach the greatest illuminator, pulled asunder by separated images, now moved only eyes and excavator's hands: he gestured our way forward.

The deep-livers, helpers, the dark forms outside pulled Sassafras toward them. Holding his many parts within the cloak which had covered him, they dragged the lord of misgivings through the channel opening; and the light flies rose up, penetrated arm holes and, entering through the cowl, crawled to the centre so that light shone out from our departing lord. In this way, the task of these deep-livers became more difficult still; they withdrew first one and then another tubular part - and the attached muscles, viscera and glinting steel vessels.

The head and the sweet eyes of the lord of misfortune still looked towards the entrance to the passageway, still flickered advice and encouragement to the mass of helpers, and the eyes too turned to us indicating our direction forward, and the images to be pursued. Such heady flights into the realm of the pit, such visions of great work. The slight journeys and small dangers now were beautiful. Elsewhere we saw the towers, lights which illuminated the earth - and visions of the rising empty air.

The deep-livers turned away. Not even crossing the threshold, they turned to the support of all the teacher's work. And there was much for them to do. The village - now ruined, the source of fine metal structures, the means by which our teacher's work was achieved – descended: his pulsing heart's desire. (This organ now lay at our feet - connected by thin strands of bleeding tissue it trembled as the whirring cylinder entered the living muscle. At the end the blood was led away in metal tubes.) This village now sank, and crossing enough light channels in its descent, we were able to see that villagers and metal workers assumed positions of the greatest striving. Their work was intensified, signs of life persisted.

The helpers, able to see such despairing gestures and the continuing of labours beneath the earth, moved out of the greater cavern space, cried occasionally for the enormity of the task they now assumed and worked more feverishly on the giant machine. Metal containers were rushed between one figure and the next.

From the tower, flashes reached out. Helpers engaged in the delicate task of maintaining the brightest light struggled without their leader to support their great source of illumination. But the very light of fine communication broke up - throughout rocky passes and under streams - channels faltered and we were able to catch sight of a winged form.

The being surrounded by the flight of beautiful creatures, starlight and the deep blue air might rise too, and, spinning and diving, cover the broken landscape. With such messengers it might become lifted up and carried, might direct their movements over large areas and, swooping over events below bring certain others to the ground.

Above all exploits birds will hover and will have carried with them hopes which we find familiar: the flight above poison vapours and ever-expanding rock surfaces; the death of heroes. Such birds fly above levels of baseness to become like the sun.

The leader's eyes flickered upward, there was something else which we did not see and his eyes followed the greater shape of the central figure in the open air as he bore the pain of all breaking hopes and rose above our suffering and that of villagers, the disturbed rock lords and departing grass maidens. This figure's shade fell on the ruined tower.

Below, figures we had passed looked up. The forms - at the base of cliffs they lamented the passing of massed crowds of travellers, flying creatures and the whispers of figures beneath their feet - such standing forms feared the approach of terrible pursuers. Thus disturbed, they remained silent during the death of friends. These eyes, too, had seen the gathering of the travellers, the passage of others up rivers to the meeting place and, in distant regions, the rising from water of our silent friends.

Some figures had been attracted by the Family.

Illuminated, examined, The Family, subject to scrutiny from deep-livers and that of our departing lord, had inspired such hopes in the crowds in wind-swept caves by the sea that now, these figures, massing at times in the shade from birds, had joined the search in the sky. Terrible indeed the crying above our heads - down-stroke thrusts and the cries of great suffering as flesh fell. The fall of feathers from their necks and beneath, wing surfaces shone in rays of sunset. Each reflected colours from forests and lakes beneath. And this affinity for the darkened passageways between trees sent shudders between those able to see through channels to the evening sky above.

And the sun of our sorrows became vividly laid out. Such a whirling host above the land - flashing dully fired wing-strokes amid tuned and momentary pulses of light from below - caught each needle of the pine trees in forests and the lapping of darkened lakes. These might then be reflected back to us with perhaps just one or more change in emphasis, the selection of certain truthful aspects or change in shade.

The sorrowful visions multiplied. Birds of destruction hovered over smoking remains. And in journeys before we met, these beings present at the demise of so many friends might be in such close contact with the rivalling forces that they could be said to bring about, by their sympathy alone, the most terrible outcomes. The winged harbingers spread doubt abroad and flashing darkened colours among themselves caused so many to turn from us as we progressed toward our first meeting with Friend and her First Leader. In the caves at the edge of the sea, the whitened figures of outsiders now congregated. They sheltered from storms breaking over blackened rock. (These rocks, originally marked by green and yellow whorls, the mineral transparencies through which light paths might pass, became blackened by spray. The task for any leader included breaking free such dark accumulations.)

The despairing outsiders cried upward too. Cast out by their own doubts, in outer regions dying horribly, fearing small changes and the rise of wind-blown leaves, the light underneath - these sad ones failed to rise completely. We travellers continued. And at times we were able to recognize the separate forms of inhabitants of small and water-fed growths.

In life we had passed these figures by remnants of their fires, while warming water in holes in rock walls. We saw these were now made pale red, purple, gold. Their walls were sculptured. These figures would have worked into each surface ideas of their own endeavour. Where possible, travellers would examine these forms and in evening light raise small discussions with their makers. At times it was possible - staying a few days - to enter many conversations freely with just one suffering mind. At such times these figures rose, sank, disappeared into the rock itself. Certainly the sorrow grew gradually, sometimes it grew together, even in groups. Echoing cries could be heard whenever a traveller might need to depart and the substance of these discussions then drifted out after him from dark cave recesses. Amid the trickling sound of water, faint echoes would flood over him. Other travellers might complete the description. Sounds could echo still.

From cave mouths, dark visions were visible. And the birds, rising and swooping, would fly in and out. There were bloodied attacks from forms beneath our feet. Beautiful Seeker rose at one confrontation. Falling to the ground once more he shook in his agony, recalling certain events in wastelands. There was bright pain, a crack as of the backbone breaking, and the vision spread rapidly outward. Singing in the ears.

We rose from the ground after a great period of time. Looking about us, all forms departed. Into the darkened skies, wings beating hard and with red eyes visible whenever they might turn their heads as in one more attack, these pursuers sped off. From only the cave entrance now were dark forms to be glimpsed. Certainly our hopes and the growing vision met with the enmity of harsh dissenters: only at times had meetings with the outsiders met broken replies we were able to recall.

And at once we saw the substance of our dying leader's struggle.

"Go!" Sassafras managed to say and we turned for the last time from the dear and broken form.

CHAPTER NINE

We rushed forward. With each pace we came upon different images. We focused our minds on the central figure in need. The suffering figure of the open air, casting about itself gold, became hidden. The glorious and upright figure likened to many men raised in beauty, shining, wonderful. And at once, the winged form beneath vanished and we were left with the single appearance of another.

Love increased for who would be tardy, hold to broken forms elsewhere, and rise no higher when the sweetly needing helper and wonderful worker might show us his joy, might embrace with those enclosing fleshed forms our bodies and raise us too?

We ran faster and faster, rising in flight as through upper air and fought with fears and dangers gladly because one such figure exposed immense need. Where were the wishes and hopes of our great teacher, where too, the work from beneath the soil?

And all of this great exploit converged on one point. Other forms, bright but now in shadow, crossed our path. To right and to left passages led off, descended and rose to greater heights and to galleries. Beyond certain of them flickering lights of channels arose and such were these vivid distractions that we might wish to follow them too. Oh, wonderful world of these imaginings! Each form clothed in white could show its sweetness perhaps to one of our number and perhaps too to certain less brilliant forms resembling ourselves and moving slightly wherever passageways might intersect. And the gestures of these other fellows showed that they could seek our ends too, that with calculation and their hope they might uncover the framework of such galleries and intersections for they drew structures in the air, raised level upon level by their hands' movements and so indicated this and then another passageway to their own lord.

Winds whistled in the depths of these channels. Such droning reverberated in paths of greater widths, it shrieked and echoed elsewhere; these passing chords resonated and the whole region became a moving musical form. Passages forked, they passed to left and right, crossed and rose, descended deeper. We became guided by such pervading sounds. We ran on faster. We pursued the suffering figure of the open air.

And where turning life could form, Sassafras, our wonderful teacher, had controlled and structured others' deep enmity: the envy, avarice and fear among men. Rising, greater hopes were embraced and deepest dwellers rose to the air, floated in the air and grasped at slight fragments passing their way in warmed winds.

But the damp and cold currents of air circled at greater depths too, gave rise to increasing fear and we heard only the slightest droning now as of a great number of men rising, the movement of insects - or the flight of winged creatures resembling birds.

We had hastened toward the great worker's side. We had passed through territories under disordered threats - no one daring to invoke his name - while these others, providing simplest food, aspired to a greater hope: the condition of gentle winds passing through body hair and through the greatest canyons in other territories. We had run through burrows.

Now for its own protection, an ordering is felt even in the glowing rocks, and we might approach such heights, and we might fear, too, for the greatest threat of all. Of necessity now we seek the origin of the dream.

The purpose might be made clear. Growing from some diffused point the form would convolute, inflate, revolve inwards. It might leave behind one bright path or many, and turn, be different and show some new colours. In this way we knew that to be part, we were to struggle, aim for the safety of the dream, protect, aid, and give rise to the hope ourselves.

And there was some service we could do to the greatest illuminator. Already Sassafras had proved unable to recall close contact with the worker; he was unable too to penetrate the pit itself. Already, certain of us had joined the communication between deep dwellers and these helpers. At times hands and certain features of Perception and First Leader were visible in distant passageways. They directed certain helpers, shielding their own eyes, and they moved toward the tower.

As we ran on into light passages we were able to glance back, see the dismembered form, and at times glimpse what now was to happen to so many parts. And the deep-livers in the cave itself, the darkest figures now massing, consumed this new material. At times an extra limb was seen protruding from a dark form. Thus did additions become assimilated and continue to give assistance: Sassafras' head and dark eyes protruded from another's distended back.

Through dazzling bright lights in the greatest gallery, the occasional sight of a giant figure was sensed. The huge figure towered above everything and gestured to others unseen. We were smaller than one finger on such a mighty arm and were it possible for such an apparition to cast a shadow in the bright illumination we would be enclosed in its partial shade, certain of us - Wisdom, members of the Family and the Victor might then be within umbra and would look up to the largest gesticulating form, become swept up by the draughts from its small movements.

And by moving to the end of the passageway we caught sight of a shoulder and the side of this gigantic figure. The face was hidden in the rock canopy above. At levels in the surrounding alcove, openings from other passages and wind tunnels could be seen. Through some, very bright light stabbed. At others the wind circulated, touched and cooled those walls glowing with ashes. The ashes fell, caught at folds in the figure's robe, singed, scorched through to the skin and marked scars at the places where larger rocks themselves might fall.

Each traveller was reminded of certain finest outcomes, the work of great multitudes and the delicate efforts of exceptional souls. The form turned: the beautiful captive. And in the light from the canopy, brilliance like that of rain could be seen.

This figure was surrounded and made perfect. Where the light fell most brightly, the slight translucence of the skin showed pulsing vessels. There was delicate movement on such a giant form. At each gesture myriads of the smaller and growing forms moved, joined. The winds rose in ascending passages and figures formed gradually. In pain.

Pain. The figure's giant hand moved to change great weights.

Our eyes, then adjusting to the light, saw, surrounding the figure, balancing beams which moved and rose above our heads. They rose in rectangular arrays, they formed patterns; we could see the changing vertical order. One weight swung against a horizontal beam. Each conjunction, the rows and rows of metal counters, formed parts to be exactly calculated. And we were set at once in a very reverie. The movements above our heads caused an unseen eye to flicker brightly beneath glowing rocks. These visions bloomed and gave all who saw them - the Family, the Victor, Perception, Beautiful Seeker - a most intricate model of thought. And we were glad of this brief moment of clarity. The lonely collision of rocks in bright sunlight filled our minds. This figure caused us then to fly with the circling wind, and the small crevices cracked at times and the sun set.

And the dream - avenues through the bars, flickering passages of light, the broken fluctuations; one proposition and then another parallel view; bright additions and the same relation repeated; the smallest way that one great force and interest - circling birds - might so disturb the dream became rapidly absorbed in the most beautiful pattern. Such disturbance was noted in the upper reaches, moved across other rows, descended the columns and caused very rare connections of the great weights. Vibrations spread, all tokens responded. And Beautiful Seeker became stilled by such a display and the movements of the Victor slowed down until only at times of major change, when greater weights moved and countered others' small progressions, did he then stir; there were rare chords and sympathies.

We could examine the nature of the threat and the nature of this beautiful region. By small steps we were able to study and understand these preparations. Certainly, particular configurations recurred whenever the number of years that Sassafras had spent building the tower became displayed in the lower rows (we counted the small contact between adjacent weights - this pattern included, too, what we had seen of the origin of the deep-livers).

But there were many juxtapositions which we were only able to guess at. By making such hypotheses we judged the meaning of that greater part of the figure's activity. And the constant emendations and the gradual refinement indicated that, in the largest part of his array, the concerns of the great exploit itself were reflected - and there would be too, the intrusion of all things hostile: the turning of greater influences against the

Illuminator; the dangers of fire and of rivals to the Digger - and the disturbed vision of powers that lords beneath the soil might represent.

And yet there was only a region where we could agree. This alphabet of patterns, ciphers - such encompassing ideas - beguiled us greatly. Where could greater need be found? Caring travellers were able to see such a place of service, there were slight reflections of their own complexities. The arms and hands moving above us became faster and more finely placed and the movement of smaller objects became reflected. And we might have seen then a planet round the sun, and insects that fly in the wind - and pollen to be raised. There was only the slightest occasion when the figure's gestures reached out and the unseen could then disturb whatever we might see and at times we called joys to bear too, moved our own selves occasionally and discussed differing interpretations of what at any time could be seen.

But such disturbances were beautiful too and only in these overlapping patterns - obscuring the sun - could our little hopes rise higher and so be fully moved. Some amongst us felt that such a full examination was now called for that the beauty of these movements alone could exercise us completely and for ever. The gestures of Beautiful Seeker reflected the careful placing of greater and greater balanced loads and the efforts he made to communicate with the figure itself were elegant and ordered within themselves; wanting in nothing that any of our number could bring to such an understanding and certainly encompassing the whole range of our fears. In this way was formed the summary of our separated conditions, not one tremor in the night could have been excluded in any detail.

And our leaders were able to bring about some response. Measured against greater joys the slightest shift of our happiness might always pass unseen, be heard only slightly through the avenues of dark and straight trees, be caught up in

90

the wind circling and so arrest the eye whenever the sun might shine. But these moments while known to the greater figure caused only a ripple of changing colours to pass. The colours spread in waves from the nearest part of his form. At times he would hesitate and rapidly change some single part.

Rays played on sections of the metal rows. The weights there glinted. Other rays stabbed out from the rock crevices, they followed all changes. We were able to see the small effect of our disturbance: it shimmered outward. In delight, we responded. And other close workers could be involved and the degree to which this form might be aware of all travellers became the subject of more oscillation rippling outward.

First among the interpreters was Beautiful Seeker. The survivor had vividly expressed our own pain. He viewed the movement of weights from above our gallery - nearer, then, than any other to the figure itself. But others positioned at his suggestion caught sight of enlightening juxtapositions. Our efforts increased.

Only the danger to the Digger and our slight aid - small eddies float down to the ocean; certain partly formed insect growths assist large trees in developing leaves - such influences could cause labours to be interrupted. First Leader, examining corners of the giant array, suggested even now that the reflections throughout our journeys flashed occasionally before our eyes - as did, certainly, the sense of Final Journey's union with living trees.

These influences spread outward. We were to attend and to join in celebrations of sharply disturbed and dangerous actions; bright charges would reach across the brain. Blood would flow, cutting edges would then cause the greatest pain and to this anguish we were to be attracted. There was to be happiness at the sharp blow to the head, joy at a threat to life.

And the brightest moments might grow. If perhaps the Digger himself, not quite aware of his peril, should turn to the collapse of burning outer surfaces, the inward rush of glowing rock faces and the close approach of wind-etched vanes; at such a moment, the sweetness of burning and once stilled nerves - (penetrated by light and by heat; torn by the raw scraping of heated cutting edges, the collapse of blood vessels; torn by steam penetrating the flesh) - this sweetness might then rise to propel the greatest exploit so that its separated reaches, the small and tranquil passages, would become bright, become crystalline. And the great endeavour then could rapidly become ice-cold and hard. Beautifully, snow-white passages then would spread through lands and into mountains.

The air, freezing, would cause small frosted particles to form and where cracks might occur the whistling of thin air through closed pathways might freeze all life too. Beautifully it would make progress through veins and into channels and in the brain. This outcome would be welcomed too. Pain was greatly to be desired.

We rose to our feet. By our repeated movements we were to compose our response, amplify those influences clearly understood and cause what refinement we could to the pattern itself. We were to assist straightaway in the work of this endeavour.

Only the slightest tremor came in response from the beautiful figure. We rushed up to higher galleries. In some way we might be able to speak to him directly and we thought then of gazing into the eyes of this close worker, a companion of the Excavator, one lightened by the Great Illuminator as not even Sassafras, our guide, had been. For the teacher had seen the shadow of a figure departing at certain rare moments, and he had worked with great application at moving earth from the first trench that such an obscured figure had once made.

Sassafras, then, had only rarely seen the close workers. As we ran on, finding a rising corridor, we reflected on the movements of zealots and the ancient singing; on firelights in the far distance, the illuminated discussions of these elevated workers. We ran into the bell-shaped gallery at the very top of the figure.

Around a central dome were the discarded remains of recording devices and banks of coded counters. Such might resemble the sections of the greater array, but certain repeated weights suggested that the sections fitted only smaller parts: the lower pathways and at times certain peripheral encoded gestures. The air was chilled.

Winds howled from the small passage leading off and the violet light from the depths of lakes spread out from the dome. Whenever we approached, the icy winds circling the central shape tore garments into filaments. Standing where these circling winds might carry such cords to frozen figures by the walls, we succeeded only in pulling individuals back to warmer outer regions if they were themselves able to understand their danger, were not so frozen as to fail to grasp the cords at all, and still retained the hope that could lift them from any such outcome.

Winds circled in the hollowed spaces and glided over the ice walls, carrying with them the smaller droplets which needed only some surface - the face or other skin - to form large ice crystals. And where blood might then flow this too froze and red fibres then ran through the white. We became frozen to the walls, we fought, we fractured many ice-fibres. Echoing whispers rose from the side entrances and alcoves. Terrified, we struggled to surround the dome.

Eyes peered through entrances about us. At times down such dark passages, louder than the winds, the sound of crying could be heard - and sounds, too, from the tops of trees.

Where it proved possible, darker forms arose. Now no longer able to view the rise of life from vapours, we cried out too. Rare delight at the penetration of trees. The moon shone; it stretched between grasses - there were islands of trees, shrubs, the hedgerows.

Above the ice and below, water trickled in new tracks across the earth. Beneath the sheet, bubbles coalesced and ran wherever a crack formed, caused by sun during the daytime, during the night by slight movement of those animals still alive.

In the cold wind and able to see an horizon slightly glimmering the thousand lives circled. They penetrated the smallest points where moonlight flickered, where small sounds reverberated and where breathing could be heard. Each slight whisper rose and turned in the night air and the flight of thousands whirled unseen - with this wind came harsh visitors and pain. Fingers stretched out and the night shuddered as one, froze. Now the avenues between frosted grass blades and the nests of preying animals might be entered into; and whispers heard. There would be harsh breathing and glints from the corners of eyes.

And cold visions all over could then be seen. Forms gestured through shuddering trees passing through branches, and between many leaves.

At the centre, at the point where harsh winds met, frosted metal glinted. Round the dome, the winds turned and ice formed in the air. The winds rose higher. Ice particles froze instantly and flew past, cutting all exposed skin and tearing at the lids of eyes. Round one side of the dome an opening was seen.

We looked in. Here were the eyes of the prisoner. So frozen that only the slightest movement was possible, was the delicate head of the huge and beautiful figure. Eyes with the lids partly closed stared into the dark space. The lids, over which frozen cascades of tears bulged, were pinned by lashes part open, part closed, for this figure was imprisoned by cold. And yet there was life still to be seen in the sudden crack of ice as the cheek might move; the tremble of small liquid passages from the

94

mouth on which the Victor might stand; the eyes into which Beautiful Seeker, raised on the backs of many helpers, might look; and the wound once opened on the brow.

The wound pulsed and at times the icy surface of blood cracked with greater movement. Thick fluid, before it froze, steamed in contact with cracking ice. Mounds rose and the wind armed with ice fragments cut furrows into scabs and scars. The brow shuddered.

Tears flowed beneath the thinnest frozen surface. Matted hair was thickly joined in heaps, wetted and frozen, where the opening met the mound of the floor.

For the calculator tried to speak. Seeing us he made slight movements of the lips, and where warmth from the breath had kept an ice passage clear, a slight whisper of air moved outward to meet only the coldest winds; it then caused its moisture to freeze to beautiful particles. Each icicle then struck the face violently.

We were unable to speak or even gesture in front of such eyes. But there was now so much that we wished to ask the adapted one and this - the imprisoned part of the beautiful calculator - was subject to all the pain of each of us and these sorrows could be seen in his eyes. And the great rock walls, the confining space and the degree of all freedom thus arranged might then be so adjusted that the finest expression of function, concern, joy would be gestured in still air.

Our great teacher's work was recalled in the appearance of the tasks of striving metal workers. There were greater efforts still. We were held by the beautiful fantasy of a thousand wonderful nights, the striving of figures from the deep and the imagined wonders of greatly creating visions. All that surrounded this wonderful worker, which held him captive and prompted his very gestures, could have risen from this work, been brought to completion by the teacher. It could thus express desires and intentions which we were aware of, the many other ideas which time had not allowed Sassafras to teach and the way in which ideas met in the brighter hope, the greater will. Light shone brightly now all over a once dark valley. And the figure's beauty shone in suffering and the light only flickered into his great eyes. Where we were able to suffer too we joined his greater pain: the shifting balance of a great excavator, the modelling of this exploit and the willing acceptance of all such anguish from outer regions, every broken and bleeding tree's suffering and the manner, too, in which men die painfully.

And the cold winds bit hard into the beautiful face and he was able to make just one surprisingly low cry (instantly cut off as greater hurt flashed across the delicate features).

Colder winds moved round the chamber swiftly, and there was grief from each broken soul from the village and from the dying forms beneath. Now cooling lava and the boiling rocks plunged down; and within them died workers skilled in the making of dreams. We rejoiced at this influence of the teacher. Now the greatest form possible guided and suffered with the endeavour. And the fearsome faces turned to us, too, reflected the darkest view of the world which moved outside, rose; whirled with bright, dead images. And the light there might stab downwards, all here might suffer and the same deaths might greet us and all other workers as had befallen loyal artisans, great designers and the expert workers in iron and in steel.

In an incomprehensible world pain entered speedily by channels, turned in the wind and descended upon the great, the grateful for suffering. The figure spoke:

"Strangers within the earth. Ice in distant places."

We trembled. As he spoke, the ice fell away from the mouth and the smaller fragments were carried violently in the wind, later to cut into our flesh, break against walls, and set up wind-carried ringing tones. And the calculator's words were swept away by winds and obscured by resonances:

". . . The light-bearer's work. And so control all disturbance. To spread outwards."

But the calculator was not speaking for us. The smallest of the other figures, white and seen only briefly, was caught in a stranger communication still.

The giant before us showed that he saw down branching and distant pathways, he shed each suffering dry surface in turn and wherever the nerve should become exposed, his touch, taste and all aspects of memory and imagination would become one completely.

The figure's vast and beautiful form, part of the work of our teacher, was now refined and ordered by such pain. The suffering of the whole endeavour developed each fibre in turn. We looked to the small features of its skin. Below the ice, the surface itself shimmered. It moved in wonderfully flat planes, it glistened and, when the lips moved in speech, there was the hint of the rapid and elegant rising of metal parts. At times we had seen the regions where figures arose and the functions thus ascribed, varying, amazed us and caused us to fear. Then all that is wonderful might arise too for the condensation could not be visualised at all and the way in which this creature lived, its approach to harmony and the acceptance of suffering grew from the accretion of unimaginable agonies.

The new mind growing could take on stranger forms. The wonder then was that it should express beauty and the manifest increase of the form. The whole might then become far larger than its small origins and the enlivening passage of brilliants down avenues. Taut fibres of nerves would then cause visions larger than any creation.

At once certain essays rose in our minds, dark and deep structures produced suffering forms. Nowhere was their own pain so beautifully felt. And the dreamer, the enlarging endeavour recoiled less and less, was able to recognize and to

97

amend where pain might be deflected. He so adjusted the growth of the Sufferer that whenever the larger anguish floated and rose he was then, lovingly, able to turn it to even greater excess. The new form increased.

Empty and echoing caverns, the sharply indrawn breath; wonderfully there was a larger hope and the capacity overwhelmed even loving strangers and the helpers all around. The whispering figures floated through their tunnels. These sorrows spun in the air and the whitened structures became elevated and rapidly spread outward. Wherever these distantly upward moving bodies might amass their pain, the greatest fantasies turned deeper peril and suffering into something moving and flowing.

Fortune turned over and over, growth continuing, its elements frighteningly obscured. And the figure strode out down those passages and the caverns beneath our feet. Darker and darker channels turned in on themselves, grew in size.

Certainly there were other forms which we had seen on our journey through channels and these had crossed and re-crossed our path. Thus was brought about the development of beauty. But a single direction could not be known from other regions. Throughout dark journeys the suffering figure in the depths took within itself the great sorrows, the importuning of shadowed forms and passed upward through more branching ways. As pain settled in layers his form became stronger. For each figure, tears welled in dark oceans. Ripples spread outward, as they left the shores wavelets developed in cascades. In darkness over a sea, the wave would rise to storms and sink to whirlpools. Within, small figures could be lost and tears then added. Pain overwhelmed the last heads slowly. Cries should then be heard.

And figures screamed for the lessening of their sorrows and these too were encountered - by turning darkened visions, at times by stabs and cracks. Strangely, these penetrated the sea's surface as lightning might pierce the waves.

The dark seas and cries rose higher, might be collapsed in sounds from birds that spend their whole lives in flight, that live away from land. Thin air and rain. And small shining lights could appear on the rising surface. Darker turns then might enclose even these. Such cries are solitary.

The creature strode through water under the earth. It moved in channels and where the water could boil to the surface other cavities led it down. It would fall wherever light could cross it in narrow beams, beams causing brilliants and penetrating the spray. Growing so in the light was the figure of sorrow. The growth of the darker form was necessary still: the dream, layer upon layer of the finest sensitive supporting tissue, the growth of the ideal.

At the edges of seas where no light rose, where the birds attending the movement of waves - flightless, sightless and at times adapted to devour only their own kind - the birds would move on greater waves, move in circles round the striding form and inflict wounds conceived in emptiness. Thus all that was necessary might be stripped from the growing form, and moulded in pain it could grow beautifully. For the need of the endeavour was so great, and the service it might be able to give so great too, that mere agonies of dismemberment were never to hinder this progress. Pain might fulfil great need.

The figure grew beautifully. In channels it could then stride out. Where the cries of other sufferers might echo and be carried by the winds in passages with water rivulets; aided too by greater excavators still and the movement of newly living shapes - there the figure would be wounded by forms which might move down darkened passageways, could breathe no air at all and could only curl round corners - thus to throw forward their greater weight, their crushing jaws. It was possible indeed for heavier weights moving to bring about change, for fears to rise, be swamped by events and then subside.

But the figure's passage was a larger inwardly changing space - involuting - and where an end might seem to be well placed at the completion of difficult struggles, it was quickly to be found that the path there opened out. At once, confronting a rock wall, it would turn over on itself, become so large as to include the whole of the former tunnel (no more than a small and straight projection on the greater floor, a ridge obscured by rock falls and certain rivulets) - this folded passage then would allow the figure to grow.

The form developed from the needs of the endeavour and especially from the essence of the small suffering creators. And the rocks themselves had deep influence. Where our wanderer might pause, these breaking and mouldering forms, the growing crystals and traces of early depositions - each energetic growth - might relieve confusion, aid the private study of the order of success.

And the structure of crystals - the small and growing bright spaces in rocks, the ordering and beautiful response of forms such as feldspars; the turning of shales and sedimentary rock - was the welcome framework upon which all other arrays might be made; and the twisted, heated, flowing shapes forced themselves upward, sideways and along. Small bright crystals rapidly cooled.

The record became, in the wanderer's eyes, something admirable. It became too his later impression, the rapid adjustment of greater weights and early reflections of broad colours representing pain.

For so great a task as ordering and encompassing the grief of the great endeavour, this wanderer upheld the structure of crystal processes: bright arrays in the curious arrangement of adjacent surfaces. The very movement of the giant before us would reflect the small dislocations that crack and run jaggedly through crystal-formed cavities. An understanding of fine traces would reveal the history of crystals as they move, with the passage of rocks, nearer the sun.

Nearer to the stars. These stars move. The passage in fixed paths is to be exactly calculated and greater movement could be possible than has been known. All will then be recorded and frequently interpreted. The movement of all awaits only application and individual appraisal along many lines of sight.

From cave entrances echoes and cries were heard. Whitened faces moved agitatedly, the broken and bleeding bodies turned toward the nearest approach of the leader of sorrow. Through underground passages, up the greater slopes, the small rocks broke and crumbled under their paces and the touch of grasping hands. Following greater whispers these figures had moved for centuries.

They cried out in the agony of hope. Throughout the passages, their cries massed to form the sighing of the wind - which could deflect a drop of falling water from the roof of the cave or cause the low sound which might give a traveller pause on a warm night, cause him to peer through undergrowth and only then move on. At all times, the noise from so many sufferers concealed distant silences. Their faces were seen momentarily but hidden by whitened garments. They called just near to the crossing paths. Wherever the wanderer might then have moved, light figures would so throw themselves upward and forward that the earliest among them would glimpse what we saw now: the beauty in ice of the calculator himself. Others who had also pursued the sweet goal would then reach only some way towards the striding figure. They moved through their discovered waterways and launched journeys centuries long to points on the wanderer's future path.

Within such hopeful expeditions were the slight figures we had glimpsed now and again: the travellers at the end of their great journeys bearing with them unimagined pain felt by millions. Greater still were the sighs and expired air from the untold numbers who journeyed, struggled and fought on their way upward only to miss by the shortest time possible the passage of the wanderer.

The ways in which their journeys might go astray were so many that we all paused at their contemplation. Judging the progress of the giant figure incorrectly could cause the pilgrims themselves to arrive moments late at a turn in the rising path or else to miss it altogether. A wrong final turning might reduce to complete failure the efforts of hosts pursued through centuries. And there would be other bodies, as well, for the calculator to feed on when he arrived too soon.

These sorrows and uncertainties were expressed fully by those who did reach the great listener, and at the repeated calls from the channels surrounding his head echoes and whispers of uncalculated pain drifted toward frozen ears and eyes.

The wanderer was now imprisoned. Long years had accustomed him to his purpose in captivity. At a particular reverse, the passage would have brought figures scurrying to meet their Sufferer, perhaps to touch his hand. And this great form would have penetrated the small halls and corridors, the twisting avenues surrounding the cavern. Desperately at first, the wanderer would have tried each passage, as a large and wounded animal might rush fearfully at the larger openings, disturbing the life there and then, blocked, might rush to one and then another channel. At each turn, then, suppliants would have waited, speaking in whispers of great pain and so increasing his suffering. The light from stars and all luminous bodies amid shade would then begin to depart - these are many-coloured centres and shine transparently beyond each figure - all would then be diminished so that only his ordering might save him from total collapse. This Sufferer could not die.

At such times all rocks would echo to the sound of the Sufferer's own cries.

Finally, he had struck upward into the largest space of all. In terror his great weight had been raised higher and the armoured head rose up to where winds already turned, swept by expired air: the sighs of approaching multitudes. The cries and the sorrow drove the air forwards, freezing all as it passed descending rivers.

We trembled at the surface. We were able to see the colours and patterns of the Sufferer's own work: dream upon dream, the direction of our journey and of others uncounted. Throughout, the balancing bright surfaces moved beneath us. In sequence they represented all painful processes, great advances and sacrifices from lonely workers.

CHAPTER TEN

Among turning images, we were to move freely and rise. Perturbed effects then could ascend differently whenever the collection of these unaccustomed influences became too great: those producing turning winds, the conflict of bright, disturbed and dangerous illumination; the destruction from above. How else might the work of figures dwelling deeply approach the flight of grass maidens, other dangers and our own movements in channels; the fearful entry of terrible strangers once moved and pursued beyond all reckoning?

Where did such powers accumulate, move beyond all constraints and so float in the air?

And from the air wreak destruction, illuminate in some disturbed and violent way the melting of rocks, cause the descent to greater depths still of the village workers and their labours: the imagined structures of one timeless lord?

The machine once more. Bright lights passed in and within its metal chambers and we traced the changes that could occur.

Tubes of unmarked crystal, metal pistons which shuddered as certain blades and angled forms rotated, sliced and reflected -

and there was turning, tumbling water; its descent in arcs. There were, too, remnants of dreams in bright sunlight and those unimagined. Such purposeful movement! Traces and brilliants!

The figures moved their weights in chests towards the lower surfaces. Within familiar lights the glow of wood being penetrated and perhaps, too, of finer feelings being extinguished was taken up and moved and joined elsewhere. We marvelled at the symmetry and delicacy with which each smaller function was performed.

For what can such devices produce except some change which we believe to be true?

The subjects discussed with the workers on the way from the tower and what we ourselves had seen in the workrooms of the tower - the teacher's broken efforts; his smaller models and the charts on walls; the table models which since had exercised our imagination; the phrase caught from our teacher's speech over high winds and above the noise of his turning creation - all made evident the cutting, turning, sliding and smaller more complete changes. (Such mystery and our imaginings: blinding sight - vision between leaves.) These insights themselves caused us to stop, to raise our hands silently.

Sassafras had brought about transformations. The light that his work made and the distant passage of information in channels were only some necessary part of a great process glimpsed occasionally. The teacher had made complete explanations, the workers had shown us each of their structures. Parts of what they had said merged and our discussions had shown that light could emanate from great tasks indeed, that only by sensitive responses - in the manner of delicately turning plants, the fine fluctuations of organs of sight - could the greatest and most moving changes be made. The process responded to changes, caused fine light tendrils to pass intimately between rocks moving on mountain tops.

Small parts of what our teacher had said caused us to understand more, to visualise the protection which his efforts provided and to fear nothing for those of our number taken swiftly from us - in torrents in the passageway and when crossing land burned by rays.

For had not our teacher had contact with the changing Pit Digger himself? At the time when such a worker was approached directly the many transformations had been effected within the teacher's sight. Certainly, behind only linen shelters the work had begun and the elevation of the man took place within easy reach of our struggling lord. He then, suffering all dangers and changes to his body, became mechanically assisted (the product of his own imagination, partly propelled by the dream). Where the onslaughts from outside caused more and more injury to his body; where inadequacies threatened in any case to hinder the work he had planned for the largest exploit, the product of his invention set greater arms to work, caused assessments to be made automatically, and in all ways increased the effectiveness of limiting forms. In the company of other workers, he discussed the needs of all favoured figures, he assimilated their anguish and was able to advise and assist with the invention of systems of defence.

Everything was bound to change, his few other contacts made it clear that the principle of change was understood beyond the movement of rocks and the level spreading of roots beneath the earth, the upright reach of smoke from fires and the pulse of his own heart. A greater movement occurred which required long ages for study, and which only occasionally could be seen nakedly or nearly so.

In his efforts he brought changes into the very heart of his enterprise. Where birds might prove too numerous elsewhere, his cultivation of parasitic life from decayed wood particles spreading over mountain ranges, dried by the sun and driven into new mounds by hot winds; this cultivation might threaten a million birds' lives before even their hatching - certainly before they flew frequently to the upper air.

The teacher began such strange changes that he was able to construct single balancing mechanisms to retain water long enough to divert streams and control all excess heat. The dwellers from deep regions moved towards him most carefully. Through ages they passed within rock-cut corridors. Arriving one by one and broken, they worked only in the manner directed by the great leader. They constructed elements of rock, slid into further passages and reported on newer influences in the darker areas of cavern floors leading to the valley above. The broken influences of anger and avarice, the violent need for life became so changed; and the machine grew by these efforts, by the movement of finely interlocking parts.

The imperfect changes to which certain raw objects might be subjected gave Sassafras much work of correcting and then only of adjusting. By the observation of a host of outcomes the mechanism grew, subject to the changes it ordained itself. The development was the greatest source of dreams.

In the change between the manifest dream and all thoughts and desires there lay the unseen independent movement within. In regions, the movers might meet and coalesce forcefully. We who could visualise only the shadow of such bright occurrences saw only the effects of forces joined and meeting. All change became possible, and the power of the device could be readily consumed.

Certainly, where light was strongest we saw that desires merged to become unrecognisable. In this unaccustomed change, certain relief could be expected. Other forms rose. In the light pipes, the effect of the desires of millions was distilled. For the dream thoughts were powerfully expressed. It was impossible, if we looked directly, not to be consumed, to move like flickering and rising flames. These would later spread between branches and the ground.

What made this necessary? What caused even future events to turn, evolve, twist this way and that, grow larger and shine like the sun?

Many beautiful outcomes could gladden every unexpected wish. Or else we might not make interpretations correctly. And some of us gazed long at certain visions within the machine. Its parts rose and fell. The Victor, fascinated by the view into one light pipe near to the piston which moved within, watched as the enclosed air increased till it flowed viscously. It moved with such remarkable properties that, inside all light moved slower and slower; was almost stilled in some eddies and in others rushed forward tinged only with some unknown shade showing its variation.

The Victor then saw more than ever before. In the confusion of the images, not now simultaneous, strange juxtapositions occurred. The wonderful control meant that eddies disturbed all natural sequences, turned and uncovered the strangest patterns: cause followed effect, leaves on trees fell in summer and blood rushed forcefully.

The light from all regions moved in other ways down larger and larger channels. It passed towards the glowing centre where, reflected, focused and collected, the images were compared with others and held permanently in solid air. These glowed on the surfaces of metals - films of delicate thinness - through which iridescent colours were seen at times and which could delight the Family, cause a whisper to pass between Wisdom and the Victor, raise moments of happiness and anger in the eyes of all who might then contemplate them: First Leader, perhaps, and the figures now in the tower above.

Here was the base of the tower. Below this, channels converged, aided by forms that the teacher had constructed or discovered. These were half-adapted forms which grew from the rock or metal tubes themselves, drew their nourishment directly from the flow of rainwater through rocks and gained their fixing in the manner of plants themselves: by sensitive processes which passed through rock cavities and the fractures of suitable strata. These figures' arms and hands supported the light pipes. They were able to protect and repair all parts within reach, and their joy was to join metal to metal.

Rare beings, specially allocated to the region where the teacher's work had been most vulnerable, they fought with burrowing animals which might otherwise build strange nests near their charges, bring about decay of the hardest metal and block certain areas of light. The cries of such firm supporters would be heard at quiet times in the night.

Darker dreams were also possible within the machine. Unable to cope with intense visions and certainly not the darkest involutions the Family, examining some region near to Beautiful Seeker's gaze, had lit upon the darker moving centre. Such a form moved within a blackened territory. It greatly altered all within. Its autonomy was strangely fearsome: it moved within solids, constrained more and more light. In their oscillation, they were changed by its passing: little was left, their motion taken up by the turning form. Within the machine, reduced images reflected parts seen elsewhere. The images were strained, abstracted, drawn by other influences and only able to tremble in their singular fashion. For they were connected and tightly held, so that nothing of an individual nature, except one single aspect, remained for them - and this would be overcome by the travelling dark influence itself.

From this we should recoil - though some of us might dally longer, hold onto the sight more firmly and so progress further with the dream.

Dream images themselves, forms taking on the figures familiar to millions rose, turned, fell within the spaces of Sassafras' machine: precisely honed metal plates and the vapours compressed forcefully within. The power of such transformations was directed along the single axis of the machine.

Where could such changes lead us now? What would any figure moving within these channels become, aware of images shifted in time? Through light openings and the focused fluid beams, smallest objects stirred and moved on their own. There was no way in which these shapes, burnt and twisted, might not develop in this light. At times their movement became searching: the Sufferer, indeed, had been moving towards the machine.

Before First Leader and Friend called us, Final Journey was to be so taken up by one tree's shade that his future became sure; before this we were widely spread. Very suddenly the pursuits of separate goals merged so that things at one time very different were seen to be the same, and some of our number needed to proceed no further, became affected by their own unity and happily coalesced. The Family, at first indistinguishable, now in pursuit of pleasure, could form and reform.

Where First Leader pointed we were glad to go. In the dividing paths - intentions and desires, sweet memories and the hopes of multitudes; the tunnels, pathways, bold images and reflections, echoes and unheard-of screams - in such intricacies he was to be elevated. Later he became increasingly hard for us to see and occasionally was not visible at all.

Others were able to point to times where inevitably he must have been present - when the conversations with lone figures in the boles of trees were directed by his cherished feelings, and when ideas that no others might acknowledge came swiftly to mind. First Leader then moved us.

Whenever he was seen, no mention was made of those times when his ideas, strongly present, obscured the dearest sight of his frail form. We remember happily all those events when he spread among us the tendrils of other concerns and we were glad of such assistance.

We looked for him when we felt particularly at ease, never failing to see him whenever the wind, rustling through branches, reminded us of trees; when the water, flowing fuller than ever through fast rivers, rose to touch the lowest branches; and whenever, in the middle of forests, we came across dying trees flat on the ground and preyed on by attractive insects.

He was heard urging us on. There was clearly no need for the First Leader's presence whenever we gathered to decide on the direction to take and what precautions might be necessary to preserve our desires. Later still he seemed never to have been with us, though some have heard his voice in the wind. We are certain that he has never disagreed with our decisions made on his behalf, and if we have spoken of him as being present on some occasion it can only have meant that there was no need for him to be so - that we, so taken up by our unison, had joyfully imagined him there: he was a figure created to enjoy our single purpose. First Leader, we remembered, first directed our gaze at the rocks and mountains above.

When we had cause to look to rivers and trees, to the ascent of birds (these birds turned, feigned and brought death among themselves) and to winds moving over hillsides for future hopes, it was he who showed us clearly that from where we had come there was only one natural outcome. For we were moved by his ideas and welcomed the approach of that world of dreaming.

So powerful was this to be that certain tasks could be performed only in such processes. For by imagination was the beginning of the greatest tasks approached. His dreaming, raised above all others, indicated the way, and by this means were rocks made to break open their secrets, and the passage of light through crystals was thus finally revealed.

The process grew so that the gentlest advice and kindest motives might be imagined, and so First Leader might then be present with us less and less. These times now no longer recur and we are able to visualise him as he was - or as he might still be, beautifully.

First Leader was with us in this way at all times. The vision incorporated even himself. We knew that bright images overshadowed even their own origins and that their driving force might sufficiently account for all energies, including their own.

Such dreaming and the love of the dream! We could wonder at the power of the particular image which, rising above all levels that we follow, grows - as bubbles rising through viscous fluids increase, bringing with them original points and sparks of light. So that beneath, where the hope itself might close over our heads, we would be left with the impression of the beautiful dream. Its origins would lie within the dream so that, in fact, First Leader might never have loved and exhorted us, never might we have met our teacher, and that, in the pursuit of truth, Friend might have so dismissed her great love.

That nothing might exist!

This was the work of the teacher on behalf of our greater lord. The Sufferer, too, strode towards Sassafras' construction as other smaller figures beset him with the fears of all ages and pain of great multitudes. His capacity for pain was the severe disability brought from dark areas where he could grow from the contact of oils, water and fire in rocks. From invisible light, too.

Disturbed by the sorrowing cries, sharply indrawn sighs echoing through rock avenues and into caverns, pools of sound shimmered. There were cries from those victims of rock lords. There were pursuits in the long grasses above and souls trapped in rock falls and drowned in rivers. Others were dragged below the surface of the earth by molten rock movements. There were those broken by poison tendrils, and sucked by openings in plants and animals; more were attacked by birds. Of all these, painful sounds made hollow waves. These then became absorbed by the partial vision, they so formed the figure.

And the smallest simulacrum of a man so generated struck upward for the light. Each turn in his path showed where this worker, overwhelmed, turned from forms within trees resembling the trees, and painfully grew.

This, the first experience of dreaming, required a great effort indeed. For in the progress of forms we expected the rapid reversals of the flow of tides, rising and falling winds, and movements of great weights poised above our heads. We remembered that the figures by the caves at the sea, needing confirmation of our intent, looked for this one sign in anything that might be said.

The Sufferer, born of the dream, rising through such levels, was to meet the structures which ran through these regions, be so moved and both grow and regress, rise and at the same time turn in on himself.

For these were essences of what others might see as overlapped and confused images, and it would be hard to imagine that these should be excluded from certain other places. What sights can have confronted this form in its growth, what fierce and exciting images moving in places and planes? For we could expect that all influences we were subject to might find a simpler, purer, more compelling form to be dreamed. The true forms convoluted and reformed. Their extremities first folded and then rose, turned and disappeared in light. These images could have displayed, before the presence of a dreamer - as consequences and outcomes - the origins and important aspects of inanimate motion. The Sufferer, having all but looked upon such forms themselves, was able easily to bear derived pain beautifully.

Whether the passages which he inhabited were tunnelled by the Sufferer or were made by the multitudes of workers we could not know. They were hopeful of his passing, they reflected what could be his lot when confronted by shadows and stimulated by their echoes; they constructed shapes to magnify the dream so that, at each turning, the passage was caused to invert.

It enclosed itself then, completely. What was the whole then became only a trace and encouraged, along with the reversion of the dreamer, his increase till he could support pain from the whole endeavour.

The Sufferer moved nearer and nearer the machine. The work that he was to perform must then have been in danger. Some way in which hordes approached the victim might have jeopardised his work. Redoubling all involutions, coming closer to the machine, it was necessary to move to the greatest reverie in pursuit of the vision.

In their pain these others then took desperate measures, and the dangers from outside were then as nothing: all Sassafras' efforts could only have been insufficient against the threat the Sufferer withstood. And his sacrifice was the greatest possible. In the rise towards the light, meeting first one dark image and then another, he had proceeded toward the machine. For the greatest part of dreaming was to be performed by all close workers and their reveries were to rise beyond any origin in the machine.

His dream, facing fears, sank within him. As each new urgent demand was made by those who had travelled further than from the far sides of the ocean, further than the tunnels and light passages in distant land masses, and who had grieved all the way; who had risen fortuitously to turn this bend and enter that swallow-hole at the moment when all others might move in other directions; who directed steps correctly among untold numbers towards the turning form of the Sufferer; who, in collapse, eventually whispered the nature of all pain solicitously, and weighted his figure with greater burdens than even this latest involution might have prepared him for - as each such demand was unreasonably made, the brave Sufferer himself moved from deep to deepest dreaming, moved hands and feet while suffering more and more pain, raised eyes and gestured acceptance, motioned special depths and performed the keenest service ever to the Pit Digger's endeavour, this world untold.

And we knew that the reverie had reached to even the most separated elements - fired circles and the shadow of the self. It moved amid smaller forms which adhered and sometimes coalesced, at other times fissured and departed (in this way they led independent existences and spread brightly coloured trails). These structures moved nearer and nearer the sight; while others moved further away and to other sides. Certainly these figures moved through themselves and the Sufferer did too: he was marked out for such visions by danger alone. Great Pain.

It was certain there were paths throughout. Both upward and downward and by associations were the dream elements linked deeper and deeper. Were all pain to be so assembled, such delicate structure in dreaming could never endure, and the paths might then become breached. Such shafts would stab outward and break and mar everything, even the remote edges where it is possible to feel, impinging on the dream, the sum of inanimate force. Water would then rush in - and flow between rocks.

At greater and greater depths the mind of the Sufferer was called. Word passed fearfully among supplicants that the Sufferer was absent in a particular way and the whitened faces, mobile, etched like faces in a fire, the figures in the trees that resemble the trees, moved speedily to arrest the movement of the calculator and Sufferer. They threw fine icy threads across his path, and their tears caused crystals of ice to form and so refract and reflect sad likenesses in bright hues of available light. These passed between them in pulses and flashes that might remind all others of the cadences of speech and natural rhythms of thought.

Grief too, and the passage of untold fears whenever such light, flashing down frozen cataracts, glinted along runnels and between the icicles in caves. The wind - their sighs and the cold - the passage of this wind over rivers of tears might then hold the Sufferer in his flight, bring such a dreamer to the repose of one immersed in pain, and thus the figures could pursue his retreating, flickering mind down paths to a dark centre.

Such were their needs. It was possible for the Sufferer to construct patterns that might reflect them; to control despair. The structure moved gradually inwards; from the inanimate and once-living fringes, death crept forward. Before this spread sickness like that surrounding matter-filled wounds.

CHAPTER ELEVEN

The Sufferer knew the significance of weights poised in the air, could duplicate fears; he was able to display by reflection of light from highly polished surfaces the disposition of all major causes of anguish too. The Sufferer grew more and more adept at such assemblies. As finer adjustment, additional weights hung from still larger ones and affected their balance. This caused lights to be reflected, to interfere with those in channels and so to make grief more comprehensible as the patterns of cancelled light brought sadness closer to the surface. They allowed the endeavour to proceed from one moment to another.

We could imagine the moment of the Sufferer's capture. For the opening to the upper chamber was designed to resemble the latest in the series of involutions, and the giant figure, ascending, could not but have expected great changes as in the past. At first he would be unsurprised. Some element would then have caused him to strike out, as the first cold touch of light filaments made itself felt, and the movements of his giant hands and limbs would then have caused rock-falls and the crumbling of rocks and the penetration into seams.

But as ages passed, the progress of his reverie could

compensate for the arrest of so great a form. There were gestures of hands and arms that suggested the turning movement of machinery. Such were the chance imaginings that this dream, built upon itself always fortuitously, and always in ways beyond imagining, attracted the moving elements or else created them in its own way. The machine drove such an ascending column - heated images rising and rising - that new worlds readily opened on every small occasion.

The Sufferer's own dream reached out and spread outward. In this way, the whole empire of light could grow, might fulfil a greater function and bring about just those conditions which the teacher, Sassafras, strove so hard to protect.

All else supported the dream, and every function of the endeavour worked towards its increase. Other things not so arranged were neglected, led some lonely existence, or else passed away.

And the rock lords in their vision of the will had left out some small region. Thus the response of the abandoned cave figures by the sea added more to our vision of weights suspended and could, we felt, have gone further still.

We could see that a gesture could work as a force directing rapid upward movement. Surely, Sassafras' discovery was reflected in the work of the Sufferer himself in ordering the grief of a whole venture?

But what were the consequences if the one ascending close worker never did reach the machine? Could the whole structure now continue a great development as before, and would not the change in hope be felt in all regions too - a disturbance in the slight gestures of friends working together, some slight redirection of enjoyment which, multiplying throughout all channels and work caverns, might change even entities themselves?

Something bright and vividly expanding floated near to us at this moment.

Not one of us could visualise the origin of such a sight. Some, almost unaffected by it, would point to swirling eddies within, points where light, less intense than elsewhere, moved towards observers or else away and was shifted in hue thus causing violent changes in our spirits which might soar but could also decline - as with deep currents of viscous fluids down enclosed passages. Such a warning then disappeared as quickly as we could wish.

Surely the greatest excavator had, like our teacher, induced rising currents to be suitably directed, moved whatever was necessary into the stream of such vortices and happily made wonderful constructs come about? These tasks completed, glory would emerge from the simplest things. Wherever some deviation occurred, the adjusting hand of the Illuminator adapted all aspiration and opened other channels. These ascend through rocks and figures move within. Their work in channels, which could exchange small elements of the dream, makes slight contact with others from different eddies at greater depths. Fluids swirl between dampened rocks and broken surfaces.

In our contacts with the movement of aspiring creatures, we sensed influences which we saw reflected again and again. The workers whom Sassafras once led laboured diligently on the generation of greater dreams. Not able to create this mixture of raw, bleeding flesh, Sassafras had risen to protect the work of others even though not all close workers could be known. (The stories of their efforts increased year by year and nothing could be imagined of the furthest reaches and separated concepts of the work of these aspiring lords.)

But these workers' and fighters' best efforts complemented their work with warm, moving viscera of giant forms. In his work the way in which small charges could disseminate through sinews, and gases pass over surfaces was found. He progressed further and the workers from beneath supplied organisms that reflected closely the new functions of their lords.

And our teacher was able by intricate study and the use of greater and greater imagined force to understand more, and to effect, at last, some changes in the endeavour. In the movement of the substances of cells he could first construct that memory of all living things, and then examine avoidable dangers and the purposes to which all hopes were directed.

He made such studies from the centre of all intelligences, in the air above the hillside and close to those attracted charges in the air. In the channels of bright visions beneath, we had intercepted his images. All the matters which concerned him were collected there before the eyes of deep-living figures, they were annotated by their rapidly moving hands.

They made discovery after discovery. Flames, fixed in points of development, changed into more hopeful patterns and complex designs. Such richness only spurred him and, wherever these energies met, turned in on themselves and grew more beautiful, he was able to chart and compare, in this way increase his understanding and then inform all other workers in the endeavour. They reached greater images yet developing. How much of this was known to the Pit Digger himself and how much was left as a course for his brave worker to investigate is hard to understand, but certainly the silent encouragement of the greatest excavator had been necessary all the time in so large an investigation.

The memory of certain aerial organisms and the movement of dying larger forms - men and the self-destroying flights above our heads - enabled him to draw very beautiful analogies. Most of these could not be seen except by the examination of patterns and small eddies observed in the centre of cells. His studies increased all needs, the work of protection grew. The deep-livers collected all others who were repositories of derived memories - these had fallen to great dangers and now

120

lay dying, bleeding themselves and certainly in other agonies of recognition - and brought them, protected, to the heart of Sassafras' work. He was mostly interested in the attacks of strangers from within and the approach of alien tunnellers. The villagers, too, became consumed in their descent from the night rays. Certainly their interest in death at the tower - the assurances of the outcomes for Fair Union, Final Journey and those lost in the cataract; the movement toward the machine of all types of load - made Sassafras' own happy pursuit of knowledge of small pathways wonderful to contemplate. It was sufficient motive for continued work, for the frenzied application of all the deep-livers' talents.

Some such creatures were grown well adapted to their tasks: just as some - fixed in the rocks themselves – gained there certain nourishment directly. This technique had taken long ages to develop: certainly no figures showed memories of more protected light tubes. These creatures grew and prospered. And we might never come into light other than from bright horizontal discs: the planes where light from all channels could become focused at last. These figures were thus adapted to their role of seeing and recording - their very large eyes, growing direct from lobes of the brain, communicated by contact alone the finest shifts of danger and of hope. They became piled together: no bodies at all but their delicately touching fingers writhed. Row upon row of eyes scanned movement quickly. Such recorded shapes had littered the grass and others were carved deeply into the wooden walls of certain rooms in the tower. They had been exposed after the lightning strike and formed a great part of what the workers on the hillside had been able to tell us.

Certainly the nature of the Illuminator's task revealed itself by examination of his helpers' work and by the thought that the endeavour was supported by creatures – fearsome, devolved forms - which set us wondering fearfully what complete

121

endeavour might require the aid of such separated and developed natures. These parallels had served the teacher well. Such usefulness, and the results from the dreaming, worked to the largest effect for the singular lord.

Sassafras, though now dead, served the great exploit. His shape was dispersed and carried so as to increase his workmate's own forms, and so changeable and pervasive was his influence that the work of the exploit continued. There was no diminution of any light in these channels, nor was less pain whispered to the Sufferer from any region of the adventure. No great incursion of strange influence or invasion of foreign forms had taken place. This was now very significant, for although little time had elapsed from our entry into the region of the Pit Digger to this present centre, nevertheless, the region was so great, the perimeter so extensive that there were ordinarily many simultaneous infiltrations, and great dangers overall from the decline of hope.

At every moment legions were ranged against the adventure. Our aspiration was able to increase while still no disturbed and poisonous influence came to bear. The air was clear. We knew now how tenuously the adventure was supported, dream of dreams.

So now we were impatient to be on. The balancing calculation of the Sufferer, adjustment of compensating fears; the proper deflection of anguish to those least able to bear it, the increase of an unimaginable influence - both the teacher and Sufferer had worked with perfect application. They freely gave to the adventure so that it could only be expected that the traveller, indeed, might be drawn towards the machine.

We were observers and wonderers, we passed among these figures with hope - spared all deeper anguish of others whom we might meet. Like the forms in the crossing paths above, we could move only among light images and we wondered what was this power which so separated us from the agonies around?

It was true that even the greater workers were not thus spared.

The teacher's work, now complete, could persist unchanged after his dismemberment. The Sufferer, rising from prime regions, had approached the machine only gradually.

What need might his approach fulfil, how was this giant figure alone able to understand the needs of the Pit Digger and behave accordingly? To no one was the Sufferer addressed - no contact was made with strangers higher up, no message might reach him except from these dark figures in pain: figures moving haltingly, spiralling from dispersed defenders at the perimeter; from unvisited mountain regions. They did not yet come from the regions closest to the Great Illuminator himself. Forms near to such light might, absorbing bright rays themselves, be changed - to blackened, broken and inverted fleshy structures.

But the path the Sufferer took - reflected, involuted with increasing size - could be discovered there by specially developed figures, discordantly tuned minds and certain ones diseased; those unable to oppose the greater force of images assembling in all the channels so crossed. These, would be unable, too, to resist and control the development of hope.

Such a meditator, meeting closely the consequences of the work of the Great Illuminator, could not but respond, and, within the dreaming time, deeper images still could be met. Central forms possessed more energy, drew the imagination toward them. These forms - the local changes in a uniform impression - drew the mind as dark spots on a straight horizon, the circling of birds in a grey sky at sea.

These merged and moved. Able only to sense their presence we would not be drawn, but in all refreshing forms the Sufferer was to see true, beautiful things, fearfully too. Because each could enclose the whole in its particulars, our Sufferer, drawn on by the need to understand what might only be glimpsed, found it necessary to change radically at each confrontation.

The space which enclosed his form might itself distort hugely, invert all sequences - the outer becoming the inner - and he too would become distorted in its beautiful expansion and change.

For his form showed that matter trapped by space - space for us had been exactly uniform - was here to be deformed.

And the particles within the void became more widely separated, in other parts closer together. They vibrated in eddies and wavelets wherever a probability moved to meet these impenetrable objects. The massy bodies balked. While space might accommodate small changes, the nearer the approach was made the greater the distortions became.

Within, the Sufferer sensed no change. The ocean rocked, but its movement was sensed only by those apart. While struggling normally - the dream tied all events closer together, gave fuller solutions and was shared and in contact with other forms - it touched far distant figures. To others the Sufferer changed. The Sufferer could confront images within the dream at which all others could only wonder, and the close approach caused ripples to form. The path accommodating this turned over, enclosing itself again and again.

At each confrontation, his own form could better survive such changes in space, moving nearer to the disturbing influence.

Suspended massily overhead, the last necessity in a chain of important events was derived from the difference at least between this great worker and the figures in caves by the sea. At times we would feel some expedient might become evident, and knew then that what was profoundly felt by these abandoned figures was merely necessary here. Such was their sadness that forms giving rise to their own happiness were only slightly represented within this dream. They were separated from beautiful hopes themselves. Yet the nature of the dream eluded us. For other masses had opposed the too close approach of the Sufferer while this mass was suspended inaccessibly above our heads, and blocked out light too. We thought of the moving dark form which travelled within the compressed light channels of the machine.

The form, obscuring and extinguishing the bright hues of a translucent background, had been an image from the dream. Now it was confronted by others which took some pivotal position, and repelled the approach of the Sufferer, and of all forms like this last dark structure. We were at a loss as if the giant figure needed to know how to proceed, why and where.

But it was the function of these structures to be a framework of the dream. Moving between them, finding the nearest and shortest path, gave the Sufferer many ages of travel. He grew by their influence, increased his power and so drew from their tension, reducing their high relief and the contrast between them and their bright backgrounds. Nevertheless, the great and binding power of each vision held him in a solid grip, forced him - if he wished to approach at all - into the strangest of patterned spaces. It caused him then dissociation and the extremity of pain.

Pain. Pain which leapt gaps and broke other ties separating one particle from its neighbour. Pain rending and breaking strong bonds and producing the change of identity of centres of suffering. Small points. And the hope of consolation was broken and muscles were torn. In the turning and expanding, nothing could remain; so fluids, themselves composed of sharp points, ran through fissures, caused scarring and tearing. Blood and fire together.

And the Sufferer, so fractured, cried out - cold dark night and white stars - and within the brain small living cells were torn apart and broken tendrils shuddered.

But these separated elements, moving freely, grew and were subject to the patterns of interfering waves. The residues of imperceptibly beautiful images so structured themselves that they, at each juncture, reflected at least the outer surfaces of

125

such forms of the dream. We were horrified that within us similar essences could determine our wishes and represent the processes of our deep dream.

The figure of the Sufferer reflected latent contacts with shimmering forms from the dream. They produced what was unknown: scintillations, in bright illumination, from the greatest worker of all.

Understanding so little of the complex form, we visualised only rarely his figure working. His works, now so large and stretching through all known territory, were still a cause for wonder. By concentrating more on what was evident to this close worker we could see with another's eyes and feel him nearer than ever before. We could rise with the worker and meet larger tasks still.

The prospect alarmed Wisdom and, while Beautiful Seeker approached and expressed the images in our present conditions, these alarmed him too. Seeing so far he was even more fearful. There was some separated way in which we viewed these works that led us nearer to the Excavator. The presence of these images of the dream sensed by wavelet and superposed patterns alone constructed for us the vision of the supreme worker. We saw him from all aspects, perhaps simultaneously, we certainly moved closer to him still.

We were not the only ones to have contemplated such an adventure. Were others now attempting their own approaches, were they perhaps still in contact at this moment? For most of our journey all had been briefly aware of the finest labours and finest incomprehensible motives. Desires which extended beyond the least common approaches became important, and the territory of the protector appeared as a region where effort alone might produce the contacts and juxtapositions necessary for dreaming.

We did not know which way to progress. From the first meeting with Sassafras we had been led into this great exploit, and when we approached its protector so closely he had been broken by further effort. If we could give any part of what this teacher gave we would not remain standing, never meet with such a figure and never see the territory in such relief. Mysteries surrounded all. Quickly we had encountered the first close worker and felt his relationship to the teacher's work. Where might we now move in order to follow his path if we could; to raise ourselves, and to grow powerfully too?

And Hope spoke louder and told us how he viewed all proceedings. The closeness of the Digger had been described directly by Sassafras, and we heard other tales from the figures by the sea. Each of these views had differed except that this lord was known as a worker and gave increasingly for the adventure. All such images, like the fears we might have had, overlapped to produce new ideas, unrelated to each other and to anything that might have gone before. Indeed, the view of the Excavator depended on the position we occupied and what preceded it. In a similar way, as more influences were brought to bear we were able to see through light channels further to the perimeter and heard, too, the sighing of suffering figures in dark passageways. New aspects of the dream became evident through those able to penetrate another's reverie. More completely, the development of all hope gave another view of the worker himself; what appeared before us now as possible could only have derived from previous hopeful experience.

Fulfilling his natural function, the Sufferer had progressed toward the machine and these others, pained figures and half-formed shadows of circling birds, had in their own excess produced the increase and the flow of their own sad energies, discharging and charging their moving fears. These needs had been expressed so that all further progress to the machine had become blocked. Whatever had been the Sufferer's own best expressed pain, his efforts now were concentrated in the silent discharge of agonies distant and unseen.

127

These sad, summed, anguished moments opened before them a path leading to a greater abyss. Vistas opened and he was able to enter small and large avenues in a dark field.

Had Sassafras become aware of this new territory of the Sufferer? Some oscillation might have increased down light channels; hollowly it would have passed as a pain itself or else as movement of great weights to be accommodated by a single slight occurrence such as our approach or the dispersal of others.

But equally, the arrest of so great a motion might cause hollow sounds and light fires, might produce echoes which break bones and make gestures of lower workers fluctuate. At a distance the accustomed balance might vary. This could spread further and be reflected at massy inclusions to affect the structure the future could take.

It certainly spread great distances. We were aware that the right variation could take up perturbations not limited in time. These would spread wider and, influencing themselves, grow, fill all corners and change distant functions otherwise unrelated.

This disturbance, the blocked passage of the growing form, was the largest indeed.

We had been brought near to this point by Sassafras himself. The figure, controlling and repelling inimical forms, presented to us the most important parts of his work. Never did he cause doubts about our own position at any level within the endeavour, instead he encouraged even this last penetration into the region of the Digger himself. Somehow the work of the Excavator, the blocking of the path of the Sufferer and our certain presence were related. We looked to a confrontation with the supreme worker. But the ways to this figure were increasingly complex. The paths branching upward and along turned away from larger ones descending. We could see images down many caught in crystal passageways, refracted through light paths, turned and delayed among themselves, overlapped. They presented strange disjoints, excellent breaks in the ordered series of events and disturbances in our pattern of thoughts. We saw forward and backward - the outer cave entrances and the steel cylinders within the dream of the machine. Such disturbed visions made further advances difficult.

Progress could be helped by other means. The work of the Excavator formed the largest part of such a powerful form. This might justify all conquests and great dangers. Some unfortunate figures not yet abandoned appeared vividly. We were once more confronted by the dangers the Victor had met.

Suddenly we felt the forced intake of poison mists and saw a rising moon, large and distorted, not circular at all. Islands in dark and unknown seas.

And the seas rise, and the winds, and all that is massy and imponderable; the seas, swirling cold, unfamiliar even to the Family - and warm rivers too.

Visions mark us out. What was of value in us were such traces and the way they might persist. We could only guess at the nature of this value, for the teacher too, at pains to bring us near to the heart of the adventure, was unable at last to approach its centre.

Some mechanism responded to these traces, we were drawn inward just as dislocations in the structure of crystals will penetrate, in time, to the deepest recesses. (These will accumulate at points of most disturbance, move round such obstacles and form protective layers.) For the adventure, what consequences would follow the arrest of the Sufferer's progress? When even his passage towards the dream became blocked, what changes might follow?

Friend expressed love of the First Leader. It passed outward through air with the movement of leaves on spreading branches and in the shade contributed to our desire. We moved forward, accompanying all later discovery, and were thus responsible for knowledge of her love's object, its very origins. Thus the work of the supreme lord could be the important aspect of a wonderful personality. Known to close workers, it was dispersed throughout the endeavour.

The few traces apparent to us produced special images. We knew his work moved quickly, seemingly with insight and power. From outside, the images appeared mysterious, but the manner in which we progressed through the adventure showed us how, when completing one's natural role, the rise to ascending levels was quickly and very naturally done. Certain patterns within matched constrictions outside and the figure could increase easily, discharging many tensions, balancing larger forces which could quickly have destroyed him and calmly confronting other allied powers. Nothing greater than the obstruction of inner moving patterns might produce this desirable outcome.

We were very glad that it did. His design, which had changed a darkened valley, could present such a pattern to us. Were it possible, we might then make occasional changes, modify ourselves too, and become light, just as the sun.

Such a sun rose in the Excavator's workings and lit the valley brightly at night. The light rays stabbed outward and turned. They attracted from great distances all who saw them, but particularly rare individuals representing closely connected pathways.

Light itself was the simplest and least connected pathway - its reflections, its passage through transparent substances, and the refractions on leaving crystal became quite the mirror and object of all life. When pain and joy were felt, the very stars might perceptibly change.

And we had known such signs, like weighty objects suspended in air, to signal changes. Certain of us, too, remembered such shifts, movements before our first meeting.

Then, while we suffered terribly, we were unaware of even the need for this close approach to the worker.

The Sufferer accomplished so much. Similarly, the Illuminator, moving still, slipped further and further away. Already we saw the reason for our single identity. Just one mind had forged between us pathways beyond all reason. The Excavator had found new work in the earth past all natural illumination. At the first confrontation, Beautiful Seeker, moving among passages (the slightly moving columns between green leaves), was able to convince each figure resting among roots in the water that it might follow, coalesce and so shine. They rose rapidly and became indistinguishable. In the bright light they glistened so that - were it possible to see one figure separately - it would appear less desirable, and hasty too, and incomplete. The movement of this naked shape could then become a single path intimately closed. No concern would be lost and when obstacles were removed they, absorbing nothing at first, would then become perfectly reflecting.

Thus the Family resembled the Sufferer in his progress toward the machine. What disorders did these surroundings represent, what disorders kept the Sufferer so isolated, moving towards unity?

Some of our accomplishments reflected the worker himself: the way thought moved in light passages themselves - and the structuring of the dream.

We moved as one: we had been persuaded by First Leader in the dream to approach merger as the function of our life and had adopted so many attributes of our excellent worker that we needed to show no further curiosity about the task. For we now saw that the central matter of his endeavour was no longer in the structure of the tunnels he once possibly created, nor even in the wind and light which would always have passed down them.

The work within such structures was only a smaller, earlier

part of his task not profitable to pursue, and could even distract us from other important items still accessible, which might advance the efforts of that worker himself.

The momentary reflections and visions of the Excavator were necessary too. Were they not so his development would have been taken up by other possibilities. These ought to have been present as the beginning of great beauty at the earliest time: when the teacher momentarily saw him, when others coming from forests at the edge of dark fields, too, could have met with this developing great adventurer. No matter how great these individuals' capabilities were, each one's talents could be taken up, used in the pursuit of the task.

Would it not be expected to find gestures of happiness whenever the function was well served or some smaller outcome was momentarily better served? We looked for these traces, for in such outcomes would we not see the occasional suggestion of the still greater function and of the form?

Once Sassafras had seen such a trace. In fact, in these early days he invested him only with the attributes of an exceptional worker: he saw the Pit Digger as a youthful struggler in the endeavour itself. Certainly, this moment had been the cause of such consideration that he thought of nothing else from then on, certainly every action was forever influenced by the one moment of vision.

And we could hope for the same. Unlike the teacher, we had seen some way into the completed vision, confronting even a close worker, and we hoped we might progress further, becoming specially influenced, and so be able to visualise the structure of the greatest excavator.

Like the teacher and lord of misfortune, we had glimpsed the Pit Digger at times. For the light passages, reaching throughout his work, ought to touch each aspect of the great adventure - all spaces between passages and caverns and the mountains and streams above. Then in our glimpses within light channels, all places and times would become accessible; the accidents of the great worker himself must at times have come blindingly into view.

Dazzled, we would have examined this past and future - and rapidly all the work to be done. With few promptings from the centre of the dream we would have glimpsed, unknowingly, every aspect of the lord himself. It was no wonder that this vision, brighter than the sun and greater than could be understood even by the collator of such images, should cause us to dissociate – and cause too the reforming experienced and the regrouping. In these new journeys through the rarest air - firmly fixed and gently moving - we saw bright, shining, massy objects, obstacles in the air above and beneath us, suspended and even slightly vibrating; reflecting among themselves the light between surfaces.

The eminent and certain originator of this work would occupy a place distantly. In the confines of liquid air the images were recorded, their paths subject to the greatest changes ever. It would be possible to dream of all outcomes assembled there. The paths of continuity might bring the slightest images into contact. So everything illuminated by Sassafras' bright light moved and shifted - the pattern for such changes, determinable in the extreme, was certainly subject to changes from within. Wherever possible there would be changes like refractions on the edges of glass. We were, like our first leader, given to many of them, but were able to identify only a few.

All changes in sequence, from the machine's origin of the dream, had been observed to pass along pathways in every remote corner of the adventure. Nothing which remained constant did so in spite of these closely connected passages, pathways stretching and increasing all qualities of attraction. Perhaps something constant had been important to our separated courses, some unfelt but attracting element able to

133

cause our close approach and other certain touches.

This region of the great adventurer was subject to its own attractive quality - the pull of the uneasily identified central region. The sequence, varying as the centre changed, might be marked by the single figure of First Leader, who, existing in none, was able to direct changes in many regions. We were grateful to this configuration, marvelling at its insubstantiality and at the cycle of drives.

Our teacher, constructing necessary protection, was charged with producing the right approaches to an inner light-filled area and tested identities by the close examination of dreams. He watched - hardly understanding - as circles closed and other paths formed tighter coils and helices.

There were possibilities which the machine - able only to create the dream - could not at once distinguish. These quickly turning and connecting paths gave glimpses of slightly formed figures in a dark sky. Seen from many aspects at once they took on certain benign features - bright rays striking out too. We were too wary to interpret these lightly ourselves and sought confirmation at every point.

We had seen many aspects of the dream in deserted areas among windswept rocks on mountain tops never visited except by birds, where the sounds were of rocks colliding. Our separated traces, following light paths in Sassafras' machine were delayed and accelerated and brought into strange juxtapositions. The image of these connections replaced the earlier vision, representing greater imagined entities, explaining what we could not otherwise examine fully. We moved deeper, even with the non-existing and with other features never likely to be aroused.

We felt the excitement of this pursuit caused by a fleeting contact with the supreme worker. The faster the machine turned, the closer the bright images came and so the movement of the dark form became more exactly calculable.

CHAPTER TWELVE

On the mountain top, by day or by night, the light of a bright object in the skies might be blocked out by the great weight hanging above us all.

The vision of stars could fix us. The appearance of the dark image could only render insignificant any change we were capable of ourselves. In the great shifts so generated, our possible movement could only be very small. All other interpretations would be misleading indeed.

We were amazed that the attracting bright objects could be overshadowed by this blackness. We were moved by the fearful effect we knew it to have on the most real images and could see ourselves as we might stand, alone in the night looking at stars. Their light, capable of infinite reflection, would be unexpectedly repeated. The sky made unfamiliar by many reversals would lose patterns and others would be formed.

At the top of the mountains we could then look up to a suspended darkness obscuring large bodies.

Light escaping from reflections in closed paths might cause the sweetest recollection. Such a delicate and naturally occurring pattern of overlapping light could have caused a trapped and desperate Sufferer deep below ground to order the pain of a whole adventure in light. These equivalent pains would then cross down light avenues to interfere only at certain points. So containable, the hand of the Sufferer might affect them all.

At one moment it would be possible to gain sight of small details of the massive form above our heads. Its outline could be sensed if the many reflections of starlight were assumed. Reflections distorting any outline showed how the surface itself acted upon the light from above.

Many planes were set at angles to each other. The way these defined more and more space showed that there was no simple contact between the weight and its region of containment. Such a form would be unimaginable even if it were seen directly. Certainly space penetrated its mass in the most incomprehensible way. Processes extending outward and downward some small distance reflected and trapped light of stars.

By small eye movements angles between reflected paths from stars changed. We saw towers and the descending branched spires which hung above our heads. Caverns darker than this night opened. Each of us, seeing the form from a separate vantage point, produced a different and interesting model of the massy form. We were able only to gather some impression of size, and to overcome our fear at the vision when the influence of many experiences was brought rapidly to bear.

There were reflections present of the Sufferer's calculation. This model for all pain flickered above us. Stars rose above the horizon and those descending changed their reflections within caverns overhead. What source of the Sufferer's inspiration now raised itself above us?

Light through this mass would be changed by passage through small fluctuations in density and colour, the reflections at inner surfaces and intersecting planes. Should the object itself move or should light from the stars enter from different directions, new aspects would immediately emerge.

A beautiful picture then of the moving stars themselves. These light patterns, bearing resemblances to movement through translucent rocks, might mirror so many parallel journeys, give rise to images of strangely grouped figures ascending, and even suggest to some directions and objects of future travel.

The way these patterns could be interpreted was exciting indeed. The Victor and Beautiful Seeker, separated by a great distance, viewed these dazzling points of light apart, and where their two views overlapped a special distinction could be made between their two journeys. It became possible to decide the matter completely - that other eyes viewing from different directions might conclude similarly. Events could then be so ordered that they would account for these two travellers' bitter and tender experiences on the way to the greatest adventure.

Such a prospect could not be far from our minds. Through the irregular light paths to the deep cavities within the earth, others might occasionally stare upward, be moved as well by the infrequent glimpses of something large poised overhead, and incorporate yet more into their hopes and dreaming.

Our own journeys and those of the figures by the ocean were made exciting. These, looking carefully, saw rising and falling forms in the parallels of reflected and refracted light. They distinguished a certain interesting feature of the great suspended weight.

Some momentary flashes of this form showed it lay at one level. Its shape, too, was close to the naturally occurring crystal. (In the deepest reaches we had caught sight of such crystals being formed, in all cases the structure itself was influenced by conditions nearby.) Feelings of form could thus move the constructing hand to approximate the infinitely extended plane or the concept of the point.

137

The pure influence spread through the sky, growing and growing.

Such forms might indicate the passage of light and all events both simultaneous and distinct. This shape could represent the growth of fronts of light, those increasing in a space and a time.

And the figures themselves could see just this, at day, when the distinct facets might move unnoticed nearer and nearer, might allow light through undeviated, and give no hint at all of its presence. Then the figures assembled near to the sea would raise their bodies higher hopefully. All they aspired to was represented in the junction of certain surfaces. It could only have been seen by others before us.

They had not joined in our passage, while we, indicated by figures representing the adventure of light to us, we quickly moved inward to discover the points within the dream. And the activities of the externals were similar to the language of gestures that certain figures on hills overlooking the valleys might adopt - at night, observing the deflection of starlight and sensing, too, the apparent position of the greatest interceptor.

We were moved by these figures, rising and turning like birds as they compared each finely conceived detail. Excitedly they flexed their small muscles in growing agreement as they felt the significance of many angled intersections of light paths. Anything that might be observed by them would be deflected by shining objects in clear water pools, and they would work with crystals and polished, reflecting surfaces to change the small paths into sparks and points.

Below the surface, starlight sparkled on rock faces, was circularly reflected, until leaving from transparent stones on the bottom leading downwards. What these workers did in the way of selection and increase was not clear, but their vigil on the mountains in hollows inspired us all.

We could see such workers, in contact only with rare flashes of bright light, forsaking all company and the support of followers, caring for nothing essential to living, so close in fact to this special concentration of motion that they merged closely with it, rendered every other one indistinguishable from the fluctuation itself, cared only for the transmission of such happy calculations - and rose and grew.

Such workers could prove the closest approach to the great form above us. Beyond the pools lit by starlight, paths would reach through rock into larger channels. For all earth, leaves and trees in these valleys were subjected to the closest scrutiny, and all gesturing figures too; and the refracted starlight entered the largest calculation of all. The slightest change in the perceived motion of a planet could have a great effect even on the decay of small discarded bodily features. These rays moved throughout the adventure of light; they might be assessed and very distant workers might then act in response. These would have spent earlier days in arduous splendour, their bodies tried by great needs when the valleys were poisoned by the death of birds in the air.

Any sort of refinement could be needed for the development to interpreter. We could only visualise them in their isolated resting places and sense their exceptional functions. Those nearest to such workers told how their contact with the illumination above changed every aspect of the greatest workers' appearances.

The translated pattern would then move onward and be allowed to diffuse through pathways. Where some further interpretation was needed, all reflections would pass onwards through solid rock paths to the teacher's tower. There it would be possible to examine the growing adventure and to compare the design with the outcome; even to examine the night-crystal itself from afar.

All the work of comparison, once performed by the teacher, was dispersed among those who were immediately affected. Any adjustment occurred only by the direct contrasting of the image with the dream. Such work was performed at the surface on tunnels being excavated. They were dug by those deep living figures at the perimeter of the greatest adventure and where all other life might find its progress threatened. In less distinct regions, the essences themselves became divorced and forms were known to move ideally.

And the principle of living matter became important. It took on the characteristics closest to the needs of the adventure. Structures soon increased of their own accord. Our teacher, with such tasks before him, had taken to him more and more developed figures so that the work of the tower occurred speedily between special influences. The rapidity of the alterations followed the shimmering of divorced forms. Only changes which embraced whole groups and were therefore of disturbed substance could then have distracted the teacher momentarily. This was the way of the supreme sufferer, and if our view of his work and the figures that surrounded him became in any way indistinct, it was because of our inability to understand the movement of such definite forms in the progress of the dream. And our teacher had constructed just this in support of the greatest weight of all. There was no part that was not represented. What darkly moving shapes merely reflected, greater regions still certainly contained. We very quickly felt that much could be lost by our own deficiency in vision.

Those beyond the perimeter had understood larger functions than we could imagine. The metal workers, in their construction of the moving parts of the machine, had made great efforts to make their many different purposes plain to us. That no deep communication could grow between us and other travellers in the tunnels was clearly some deficiency, akin to our own inability to see features of the dream before our first meeting; our lack of understanding of that distant view of figures near the sea.

We were entranced by the possibilities of seeing this from

many different aspects. The different ways in which the workers closest to the great weight might view the night-crystal, its reflections and refractions, its relation to the stars, drew us forward. Every viewpoint was to show more of its structure. The effects of its form entered by this gentle, intimate way into the light paths themselves. And other hands and eyes directed unions and disjunctions. Such necessary comparisons were made by figures acting as one. In complete communion they could extend and adjust all light passing through even remote pathways. Their work, itself part of the great adventure, became part of their own adaptation. Only if they had been seen to make the most benign adjustments to the progress of dreaming could they be expected to continue; and indeed their behaviour, modified by the years of the largest endeavour, truly expressed the exploit's intimate design.

What existed with the purer form above? We had approached the exploit unknowingly. Sassafras, the leader, had caused us to join in the realisation of new origins. Strangely, too, he had been completely present when we neared the adventure; through others he had observed every moment of our approach. What caused his special interest; the dedication of such time to our progress?

Sassafras had said the important place of each interpreter in the mountain tops was taken by the close workers. We might now ask where the origin of light was to be found.

What work the interpreters took upon themselves still amazed us. We were accustomed to considering the small contributions of those that worked for the construction of the dream - and the origin of other slight processes arising from the creation of distant matter. Such remote, controlling influences might never be accessible to the part, and while we represented some large portion of our teacher's vision, it amazed us that we could find ourselves aware of these workers' positions, see some little fragment of what they were able to do and began to see ourselves as placed specially in their midst. We were to offer ourselves to the adventure indeed.

Each part of all distinct lives would be available to the exploit. Any useful feature of the thinking and breathing forms ought then to be taken up, passed along very distant avenues and so might move and rebound at distant objects. Every part then would be of use. We could sense movement through grasses which introduced all to the meeting with rock forms, to the passage of terrible pursuers and death in grasslands, to the attacks made upon the Great Excavator by those working within (these figures moved slowly over years towards their goal and importuned all diligent workers with their tales and their cries). We felt that movement and we also sensed that which caused light to fall through broken creepers into other channels: the greatest danger among predatory animals and birds attacking at night.

Everywhere the features of distant lives were to be taken up and changed. Whatever perplexing images the suffering multitude might give rise to, these could be dispersed in small places between branches through which the figures travelled. Such forms could be pulled up short at any moment by distinct traces of their origins; might, indeed, be pursued by any of these traces as others had been. This happened at greater heights and where rocks collided on hill tops. Every part of the strange endeavour was drawn together at certain intervals in the way that our own teacher had appeared to us and might thus present the pain and the fears of whole manners of thought. At such dark spots which most fearfully tried to avoid, the intensity of pain grew to blacken out all illumination, would inhabit darkest dreaming and might act so as to deflect, attract or otherwise modify movement of glowing forms. Certain parts of the dream presented themselves slightly to us as in the past. We could see light from the great structure above, note the paths that it took and observe as it cut passages vertically downwards, dividing the night sky into moving halls and avenues. Chambers were thus formed, their walls white and insubstantial. They moved and the valley became divided up, the surrounding peaks too. Lights were fixed in the positions of the close workers themselves.

Caverns and towers: processes were etched overhead in the light from stars bright with the movement of those bodies which circulate; and those which generate all rare alignments and darknesses.

The form itself could be seen as the construction of reason and partly, too, of all increasing changes. These views of what was essentially invisible came whenever we were able to infer from small variations how the light from distant sources passed at glancing incidence along surfaces transparent to its passage.

Could this form move? Was anything similar possible? It might remain fixed in the sky. The passage of reflected starlight, along vertical faces of crystal, could occur more simply only if there were no fluctuations and no change in position. The motion of heavenly points of light, when impinging on the most complex form above us, might readily admit enough changed possibilities, enough variations, to conceal all ramifications of the life below. And more, as the light made its passage through channels it was adapted and interpreted by the figures in caves at the tops of mountains. As it was surrounded by winds circling and by remains of leaves - occasionally by other figures whose nature could not be made clearer and might pass and essentially modify all images within - then it became possible to change pasts and futures in a single motion of the upper refracted light and of the machine. Light and the form were required to accommodate variations. All changes then might be subject to scrutiny from within.

What a glorious outcome! What a wonderful and happily formed structure!

But without movement other changes were still possible. The

143

figures by the sea, in their caves, attempting and partly succeeding in the work of the interpreters, these figures told of the weight poised above them in every part of their endeavour. There was sufficient chance of adaptation for the shape to have changed very gradually. With the passage of long periods it could have had a very different origin from the one imagined.

And there could be similarities with forms we had seen before. The involutions of the greatest sufferer were necessary for our grief. Whatever we had already seen would reflect on the working of the suspended great weight.

We could see swirling fluids, their contact with rock surfaces and the way, with time, cavities might form, figures rise in ascending air and so fight and breathe terribly - in the end to lend assistance; to control all others' fears. From this we could see that other possibilities existed: that the change might occur between shifting rock crystals and the movement of disturbed figures. These progressions ought to occur and the suffering giant, too, in his involutions, would rise elsewhere. What changes might this mass have originally undergone?

That so much should derive from imperceptible changes! Shadows were depicted in all mirror surfaces. The form's intimate control was to be exercised in every corner; it was connected by light, it was perhaps a dream of light. It would be reflected in work below the earth. Such similarities were slight or seen to increase in earlier time. What we only guessed at would be the refracted image in dream of our passing; the local disturbance of the traces of the dream. Where we had passed, like other objects and attractive centres we could expect the swirl of unknown colours to accompany our passage. At times these little lights might meet, coalesce and afford important junctions. Whenever the hard and massive forms were seen to scintillate, it might be that we could direct light in more accustomed avenues and adjust even the smaller channels and outlets.

Certainly, as a consequence of our passing, patterns of all images must have changed. None of the travellers would then understand any of the changes he was present to correct. Disturbances, too, spread outward whenever the distant attacks penetrated very far, when the individuals in the lowered channel met and joined their efforts.

The threat that the pursuing figure represented found its reflection in the small adjustments of the light in channels. Perhaps now we had seen what caused the deflection of winds themselves, the distortion of the natural colours of bright sunlight and the circling path taken by great forces above our heads. At all times such discharges were ordained by participating natures - there was our terror at the cave-mouth, at the burning of our skin by night rays and the perplexity we felt whenever confronted by aspects of the work of one lord and gift of a starless night. Above our heads, bright and dark clouds passed; universes, undifferentiated loathing, and the cry from deep and far away.

None but one so indicated could approach any centre whatsoever and the dangers which our lord had endured taught him the need for closeness. Such a derived position, like that of the interpreters themselves, could only suffer the onslaughts of forces closely balanced.

Certainly, the Sufferer was accessible to us - though not then to our leader - and the disappearance of more than the occasional traveller among us might show how, like the great teacher, they might be required to distribute their pain widely. The very number of the travellers was valued in this way.

Where function might determine form, the increase in size and still greater developments of the calculator were in response to insights into unfolding natures. The period of all early work was left many ages before and when the control of light itself grew so that it alone was made to perform the many functions - bringing about great changes as at the beginning, causing matter itself to form and reform under its highly changing pressure - and when all of this might be seen by any passer-by in the valley, then our most diligent worker would have been greatly changed and the further development of the adventure itself might require his ascension and assimilation. All work would then occur speedily.

It now became rapid indeed. The most important part of the Illuminator himself could be recognized. It might be necessary to decide that all aspects of this figure distracting from this function, diverting his living being from what now overwhelmed all of us delightfully should be left far behind, allowed to exist only in some irrelevant way and not at all if their effect was to hold back progress by even the smallest amount of time.

This worker rose and changed in form speedily.

Connections would be made between the light from the stars. And connections capable of all juxtapositions could be imagined in the reflected paths of light among plane surfaces. The effects that the passage of time displayed in containment - all became apparent without his knowledge. The reflections between the luminous surfaces of stars themselves could not be more multiply connected. These paths mirrored beneath the earth and in the permitted pathways in the machine - as well as in the paths of the dream - circulated and made avoiding movements about darkened bodies.

They circulated wherever one thing indicated masses elevated, the presence of other features of dreaming - and the forms which mark out single paths where all others are equally likely. On such occasions for change no singular direction might otherwise be preferred. Events and distant influences become formed just as in the moment of dreaming during the day. Glinting points appear as curves, as caustics. The Great Excavator, no longer able to undergo changes brought about by earlier orientations, determined his own influences and the path he could take. If movement was still required he would then cause his own translation spontaneously; no crossing of space might then occur. And the barriers and forbidden areas, the bright attractive qualities could then serve only to propel him.

He was able to structure his future. Everything which increased the areas of our possible action could paralyse all desires and render us stationary on a smooth surface. Undifferentiated regions.

CHAPTER THIRTEEN

There were perhaps ways in which these objects themselves could be seen moving. If they were not actually transparent and easily crossed, then at least the passage through such a field might be estimated and so arranged that close approaches might never occur; never might one pass within an attractive or repulsive influence and the world then ought to have a different appearance with all possibilities equally likely. The expression of these through lower and lower senses would be precisely what we had witnessed ourselves - at all the points within.

Wherever we defined the perimeter of this great exploit, there the influence of the self-determining work might begin. We were intrigued then at the different nature of travel throughout this region which had so many dangers and surprises. From our first meeting, where ideas of the greatest endeavour were mentioned, this nature had become apparent. Some quality of this approach to the Great Excavator seemed to explain the deep changes and unexpected outcomes. So desirable was this territory: it was different from all others as the last consequence of uncounted small variations.

We wished to piece together the image of this great worker.

Movement among stars overshadowed what natural curiosity we had in the accidents of form. Sassafras' own had become distributed throughout this adventure as an influence, a control and a guide. Every one of us had felt traces familiar to us, guiding many visions. It was clear the Illuminator was not to be restricted any more in this way. The important features were already laid before us and the inversion of forms might permit any change at all as long as the function was preserved. Such an inversion existed between the suspended mass above us and the void in the ground. Our sense of the attraction of ideas showed that all developments here occurred not at the defeat of aspiration but instead divorced from all compromises.

No distinction existed between the other regions of independence and the motion of this great worker himself. Any small structure attributed to him quickly became insignificant in comparison with the greater freedoms. The vision had sprung from the best efforts of the Excavator, had then grown with his larger control.

The Excavator, unable then to move unknown between the massy bodies which restricted our motion, looked back and forth in our time and connected those ends and beginnings which we believed to be not just distinct but irreconcilable. This endeavour supported by all helpers, generators of the dream, was to be understood partly. It had certainly been known and imitated by hosts trying in very different ways to achieve distinct results. The discrete form of the rock lords in their effort to influence others, and even the causes themselves, had foundered for these formed part of the sequence leading to the travellers' approach in the lowered paths.

Our paths had formed part of this image. We had agreed to think and act as one. We made a little progress towards the greatest lord. In the simplest way in which our separated views could converge, be compared and reinforce and cancel themselves, we saw more than others and it ought to be possible for us to respond yet more deeply. We thrilled at the thought. At every moment we could act upon some small aspect of the Excavator, and so respond beautifully. Always, though, there was a dulled and retreating image which we were ashamed to acknowledge - such great achievements brought so low. The hardest struggle was the acceptance of the position of our supreme teacher, for we could no longer identify an individual. We viewed this last task approximately and thought now that there might never have been such a figure as Sassafras and never, too, the greatest worker of all.

His important ideas would now be felt in the convergence of light overhead. Each separated influence from bright lights was channelled into remotest fissures between sand grains, leaves; and during the motion of viscera. The whole might be altered unimaginably from above. Our singularity, the exceptional influence not developed by others, allowed reinforcement of particular visions and the suppression of many truths. A disturbed thought might be possible while not yet experienced. It would be part of the greatest illumination - in the future indeed.

Could this be our influence and our value? If not, could it be the means by which we had penetrated far? Others could equally well have seen greater depths. Unknown to us these would then extend to left and right and to inner curved paths.

Clearly the channel of the profound desires was expected to respond to some primary force. Wherever this originated it ought to be among the smallest and most fragmentary features - in the formation of ice, in the nucleus.

So, in the fluid, unchanging in all directions. One small turbulence, arising surprisingly from complete uniformity, might gather very great force about it, rapidly turn outwards, and crack, splinter the universe in its increase. Where time became so speedily opened, we might instantly take fright.

Our supreme guardian would remain invisible to us. The

worker, present in these efforts, unconcerned to bring about our complete induction, would consider our own way formed by us satisfactorily. Now and at other times we would make our flight in the more dispersed medium, might glint and turn at each chance meeting of shimmering figures and be seen by all others in rising air. Glad of this function complementary to the Excavator we sought no more contact, knowing him to be absent always and moving further and further away.

The night sky turned and the slightest changes made the lights on hilltops become deflected and retrained. At times we might catch sight of the figure of an interpreter, a close worker himself, and consider the sight of figures bent low: greater forms surrounded in the light by the movement of secondary sources. These would be adjusted and magnified by changed optical paths resembling those of the teacher. At these distant gatherings, bright rays would stab down, be deflected and retrain light in a dark night.

We were frightened by remembered threats from above. We wished never to question the finer movements. Whenever the initial cause showed slight uncertainty, we would then suffer silently and alone.

Till then, unmoved, we would be subject to the slightest of breezes and the occasional movement of birds. Circling, they might die on the wing, swoop in rigid flight and move onwards, returning, bleeding - such drops constantly falling from above.

Their wings would block out light. Whenever starlight, not caught up in the reflections of the clear form above our heads might become broken, these returned, moving dead forms could cause that light to be cut off momentarily. The beautiful pattern of interrupted light would alter all conditions. Wind deflected from inert wings might rush circling in the valley, would bring with it the chill of very empty spaces, cause the motion of unseen supplicating hands.

The cold night would cause stars to stand out, some near the

151

horizon to burn with steady light. In their movement they would turn between the outline of hills.

The workers' lights on the hilltops were seen through still air. We moved to exact points where rays of light crossed. Though not the brightest points, these were otherwise occupied by figures changing and reforming; in the small light of hilltop fires, disturbing their own structures wilfully. Whenever space too might alter, they so arranged themselves that, like their companion, the Sufferer, they could turn and change, involute and take advantage of all the most important fluxes available - and not just the movement of water and the slow rise of rocks in changing volcanoes; and quakes which spread out on the bottom of the sea.

All workers could alter light patterns in the easiest possible way. But unable to change and control we were left with only our response. It was difficult to feel that all the work governed by Sassafras might be generated in this way. Certainly, remote stars would appear nearer, those already near might display intimate details, and those closer still be seen in splendour so that the night might be blotted out and the perception of pure light result from fine attunement alone. Where darkness persisted ways would be found for dulled eyes to be blinded by light.

Over the distant hills was a slight reason why change ought to occur. Now that our approach to the worker was completed, influence beyond that of the endeavour might possibly be found.

We were only able to wonder what this could be. The most difficult tasks were completed when the starlight penetrated leaves of trees and small inanimate fibres. Where else might this fine influence be directed? In all, there could then arise an undifferentiated reaction. Every part not completely touched could change in response to the furthest influence - especially now that the sequence of effects in the action of the dream could be subject to the same firm and gentle laws. Nothing in this whole endeavour might differ from our observations - and even pain and pity might swiftly become one if changes elsewhere occurred speedily enough, in the right order, or in some way recognized by those concerned with the greater need.

The only way consistency was to be achieved was by progress towards the final form. The controlled fluctuations by one medium and the changes it brought would cause the same movements - and an accurate response - to arise in even the most distant regions. It grew, and the expanding boundaries could then follow some natural law, irresistibly increase their enclosed order and disorder. And other things were to increase with illumination. There were states which we had not yet imagined and which remained alternatives to all that we had understood. Their existence, before cause and effect, changed possibilities with which we were familiar. We might then examine in unthought ways our journeys and our experience - which did not exist - before our first meeting. We sought to see over even this boundary. But where imagination failed we were able to move outward from each small event within the adventure, could see that real alternatives existed beyond present boundaries and that as an alternative to this world and this universal idea, nothing, nothing itself might happily exist!

As the last step accessible, we were glad to move towards any region of light. Whatever form this took we saw that to be partially understood it ought to possess features we could recognize and which we had confronted at some time before. The mysterious way experience had grown applied where sequences existed. In the dream, interruptions occurred which served very good purposes, and yet the growth by involution which the Sufferer and others showed did replace this ordered development. We might invert in this fashion in order to understand any dream.

And yet familiar features did exist. Whatever was nearest

might take upon itself the deepest sense. And we had responded to the small beauties that surrounded us. Whenever newer ideas arose we might look to see their cause in smaller and smaller features. This was the manner in which opposites could be formed, out of nothing, suggesting any necessary changes later. It was clear that similar reversals maintained emptiness and so, on alteration, could be known from outside. There was no final change.

The way we could progress was of the same nature. Certainly the void below ground and the crystal structure above showed that no ultimate change had occurred. We hoped likewise.

But we had come to something important. Where such balancing was possible we could see the inner structures moving slightly. Our many-centred sight of all regions marked us separately. No other grouping communicated so minutely. And we, by sensing an increased vision in regions and the happy suppression of the view others might take, came nearer to any balance and imbalance.

The close workers themselves assessed fine points of light and hid by day. But being many-eyed - otherwise possessing only reduced perceptions - we were to arrive at their strange positions too. Something was clearly similar in our very existence, our dispersed and plural nature.

The involutions possible with the Sufferer and the Illuminator himself were not yet equal and displayed a residual structure stretching beyond our sight. Cold air and the momentary stillness. In the valley, the water tumbled from the high ground and from the remains of the tower. Dead birds turned and turned again, small animals moved beneath our feet and we found more and more exact positions to occupy.

Some communication existed between us whenever thoughts blotted out all others, and we were glad of our own company while we waited, cold and fearful. Less and less moved.

We would welcome anything we could understand. What

154

might warm us, raise us where we were no longer distinct; what might cause us to unite truly and make no distinction between all our many figures would thus bring changes of a kind. Those departed were represented just as strongly, we were unable to distinguish Fair Union and Wisdom and the passage of smaller fragments of illumination. These were now dissociated, had at one time been totally distinct and even now might unite to enter all of our space.

Such figures, which were perhaps illusory, clustered about those centres of closest approach where the change of state would most readily begin. In these bright colours, the massive forms became centres of attraction and obstacles too. They had been fixed points in the development of the dream. Only passage about them was possible. All figures developing became structured by virtue of closeness to these forms. Confronted by each, the Sufferer had changed too. And the greatest involutions occurred in such a perfected figure most frequently, were reflected in the passage chosen for his rise. Where he might remain stilled was the point of a particular perfection. We felt no grief at the death of other forms.

The fragments of illumination in random motion had already been separated out. Distinct ranges of energy became merged. Sinking in brighter light still, identities reflected quickly occurring events. They continued to lead us when we needed them and only later appeared quite the same as each original distinction.

In whiter and whiter light they became less and less separated. Some source would remove shadows, dispersed and free movement would then occur. There would be no preferred direction and no further development.

Many aspects of the work of the great exploit could be seen as one. All the figures, partially formed, were fixed distantly in one venture: in the moulding of planes and cutting edges, the refining of the intersections of very sharp blades. These might slice even the finest particles in air, cause layer upon layer to be compressed and the surfaces of metal to be so smoothed as to retain charged images long after their illumination had gone.

These sequences of dreams had been of the greatest benefit, had increased aspects of our own selves, had caused our unity and had rendered us so like the moving light that we now directed our attention quite randomly. And the source of this still eluded us. The greatest worker was well represented now and only a dark night remained. As cold, as circling dead birds, as rain.

Changes could occur in the night - the passage of stars and independent movement of other bodies; their reflection in the columns of light pierced by the passage of birds - these variations might occur as a result of changes in wind formation or the descent of body fragments to the ground. Rays from distant places would remind us of the glow of daylight over the valley when the great worker was to be seen occasionally and when figures might approach the greatest adventure. We could not visualise and nothing could describe the effect of day in the middle of the night: the rise of a strange sun; the discovery of rocks poised about to touch and movements in very distant places.

Such an exploit was less pronounced in these regions. But with interest and greater progress, less obvious structures grew and grew there. What were visible at first evidently became subject to any amount of variation. Following these changes such incidents started to be a matter of the greatest skill involving chance itself and the imaginative interpretations of many others' intentions. Such uniformity became an object only after many disturbed sights arising from displacement in time. We sensed we progressed rapidly.

We talked of the first idea. We noticed the later unity, recognized the value of our own and the place that departed members now took - those who might never have existed and

156

among those non-existent, those whom we loved. Among hard massy shapes the movement of such imbalances had produced distant effects. All matter became affected at times.

The movement about heavy centres might be altered. The flow over, beneath and around, signified their occupation of no volume at all and this encouraged the greater movements towards uniformity. In the bright rays of the rising light this would account for all lack of preference.

Such an excitement from the proper positions that many had discovered! Light came from brighter stars in smaller and smaller reflecting pathways. All these stars' light joined at times. The bright rays burned through all shadow and shade; through the smallest branches glinting with raindrops.

Whenever light unfroze frosts and caught at rivulets, it became reflected into our eyes.

From lower in the valley, mists would move higher: towards us. The figures on promontories would be separated from the sea: there were indistinct colours and the vapour below. What bright colours merge!

Areas of dark persist.

The sound of metal-working and the movement through spray from waterfalls arose, disturbed the massing of bright illumination and the joining of all close workers. Cries from the river, the passage of river water down swallow holes, the fracture of metal forms; we felt the rush from the waterfall. Separated figures clearly visible rose up the steep slopes to the points occupied by the workers. We were heartened to see all figures from the recent past, from points where time might collapse and certainly they were dear. These had all occupied moments when we thought suddenly as one. Individual figures - at times these were sorrowful - bore traces of the greatest occurrences and could be recognized as early forms. Unease was felt as they approached the positions of the close workers. All figures occupying their positions on exposed hills

157

increasingly reflected the light from above. Brighter rays, very distant, moved towards us over unseen land and the frozen valleys beyond. These touched dark spots in crevices and passed over others completely. In all such corners the air would be stilled.

The shadows of this night were disturbed by the light on the horizon. Any movement formed part of the function every massy object in the dream could perform. By interchange of position these forms became indistinct, ceased to influence the development of changing structures and allowed all to progress almost equally.

At that time the brightness would come from all directions at once. The borders between ourselves and the air, broken up, would glow, too, and all causes and effects would unite. Such changes occurred again and again so that original natures altered completely. In their advanced attempts, the close workers, the Sufferer and the Illuminator might completely reverse. There were involutions in every aspect of the workers' tasks - and the great weight floated above our heads, was permanently suspended and came to overshadow those figures by the sea.

It was to be hoped for: it would control what followed. Light shone through and the rays reached out from distant lowered ground. When light rose and caught the position of any worker, that figure might then move into cover, by reflection redirect the light and concentrate it inwards.

We occupied a certain region. And the curious nature of such a space was that, while present exactly at the centre, this focus was distributed widely elsewhere. A single line might run vertically. Through the tower, the great weight too; the dream. From very distant outer regions, through all our displacements within the territory of the greatest illuminator, this was the singular discovery. And the machine might be aligned in a similar way too. What was important was channelled in one direction, and we had passed through just this line when entering into bright channels and galleries and soon met the very close worker indeed, the Sufferer.

We were supported from elsewhere. As the figure of our teacher became dispersed and the limitation on the movement of the great individual below ground increased; as the efforts of all workers present and especially those very distant grew, we, along with the focus, became dispersed forever.

And the structures of all the tales told in the outer regions, the images engraved and dear to the figures in caves by the sea; and the efforts of workers concentrating on metal and their support of what others might need to bring about change; and all failed efforts too, and all misrepresentation, and the rise of light gradually behind the hilltops; rising hope and the interpretation of whatever might be universally imagined - all this spread, rapidly, possessed no centre and was able to merge indistinguishably with small details.

Underneath, the forms mounted upon each other and on unchanged structures, through tunnels and towards lower galleries. At times they turned in agony, every one so well connected, by channels and the redistribution of time.

The circle spread wider and influenced figures outside even the perimeter and partially those in other circles beneath the earth. With no sorrow we turned from examining all failed forms and gloried in the elevation of the unknown sun.

Books by the same author: *'Hor'*   *'Corridor Dance'.*

L - #0478 - 201221 - CO - 210/148/9 - PB - DID3230614